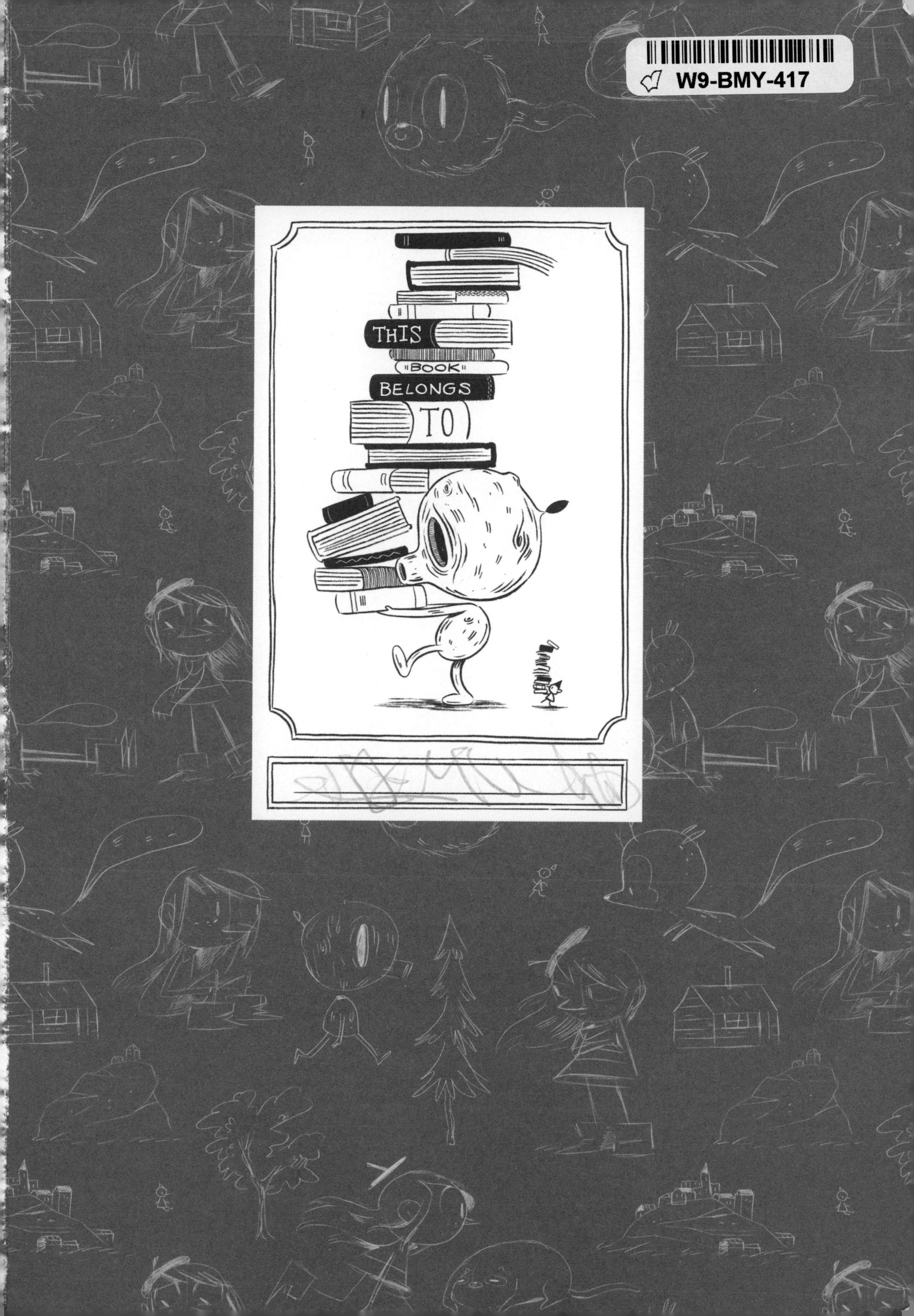
THIS
BOOK
BELONGS
TO

THiS PAPERBACK EDiTiON PUBLiSHED iN 2016 BY FLYiNG EYE BOOKS.
FiRST PUBLiSHED iN 2011 BY FLYiNG EYE BOOKS, AN iMPRiNT OF NOBROW LTD,
62 GREAT EASTERN STREET, LONDON, EC2A 3QR.

2 4 6 8 10 9 7 5 3 1

PUBLiSHED iN THE US BY NOBROW (US) iNC
PRiNTED iN LATViA ON FSC ASSURED PAPER

iSBN: 978-1-909263-79-6
ORDER FROM WWW.FLYiNGEYEBOOKS.COM

LUKE PEARSON

HILDA
AND
THE MIDNIGHT
GIANT

FLYING EYE BOOKS

LONDON - NEW YORK

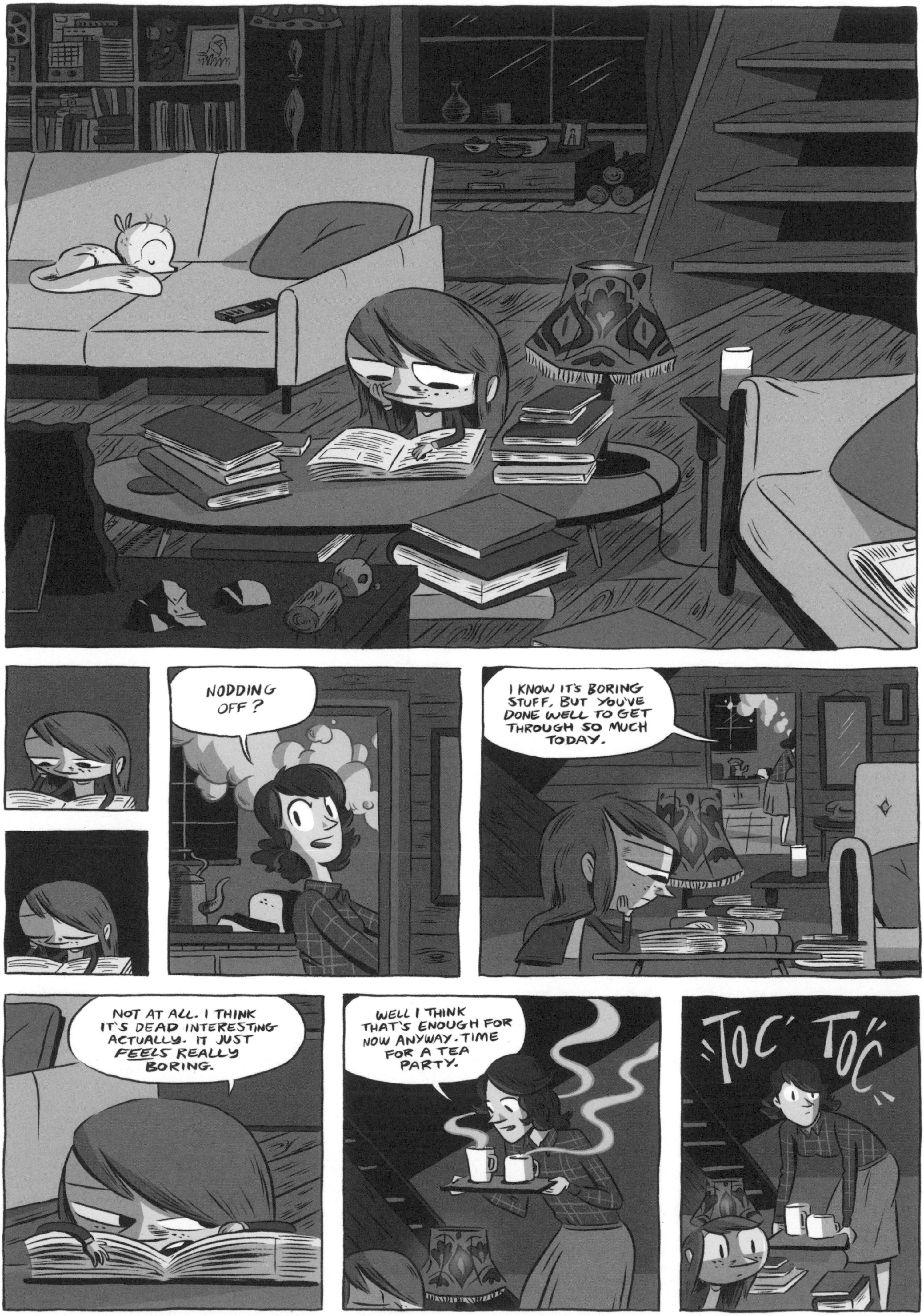
NODDING OFF?
I KNOW IT'S BORING STUFF, BUT YOU'VE DONE WELL TO GET THROUGH SO MUCH TODAY.
NOT AT ALL. I THINK IT'S DEAD INTERESTING ACTUALLY. IT JUST FEELS REALLY BORING.
WELL I THINK THAT'S ENOUGH FOR NOW ANYWAY. TIME FOR A TEA PARTY.
TOC TOC

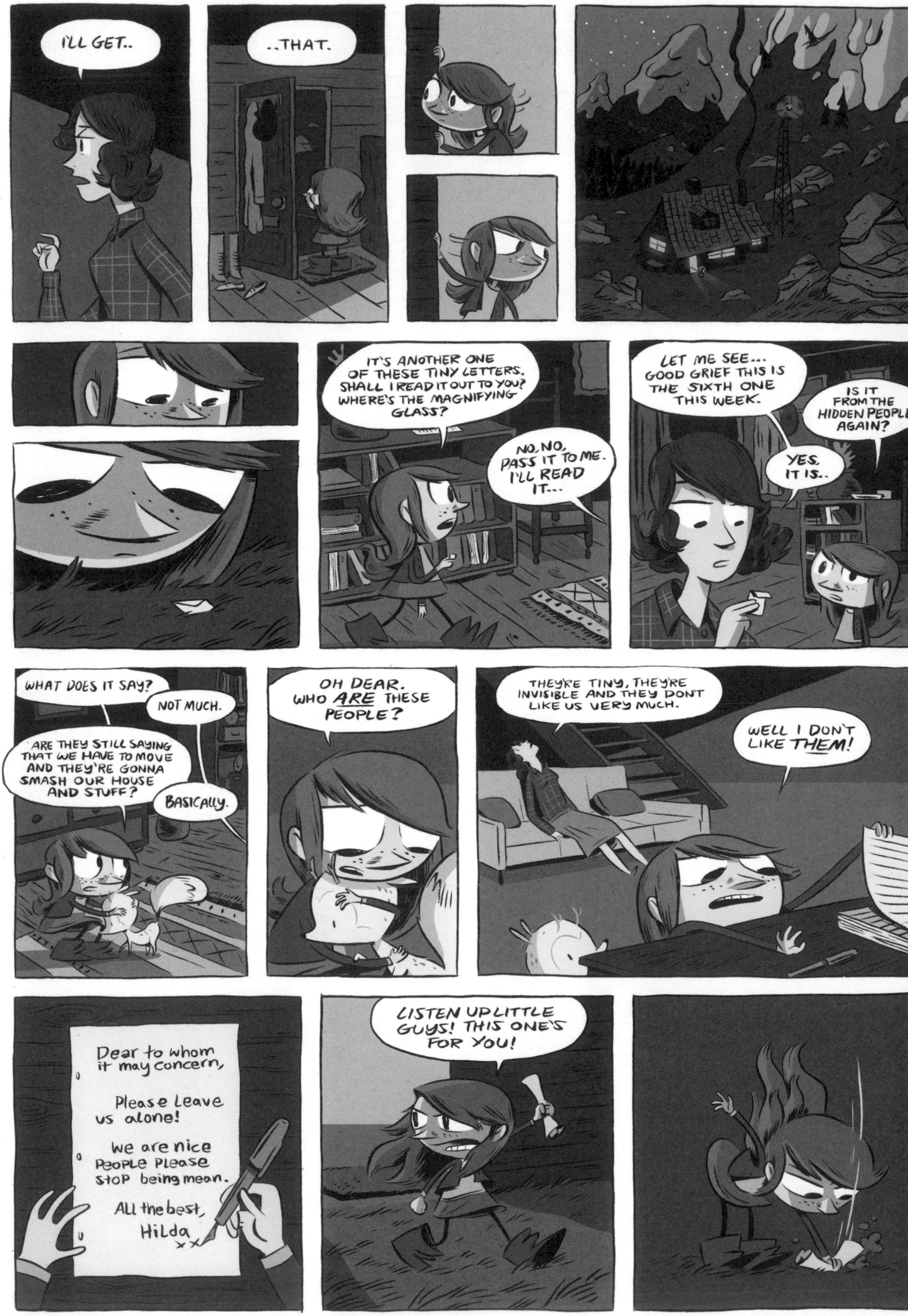
I'LL GET..
..THAT.
IT'S ANOTHER ONE OF THESE TINY LETTERS. SHALL I READ IT OUT TO YOU? WHERE'S THE MAGNIFYING GLASS?
NO, NO, PASS IT TO ME. I'LL READ IT...
LET ME SEE... GOOD GRIEF THIS IS THE SIXTH ONE THIS WEEK.
IS IT FROM THE HIDDEN PEOPLE AGAIN?
YES. IT IS..
WHAT DOES IT SAY?
NOT MUCH.
ARE THEY STILL SAYING THAT WE HAVE TO MOVE AND THEY'RE GONNA SMASH OUR HOUSE AND STUFF?
BASICALLY.
OH DEAR. WHO ARE THESE PEOPLE?
THEY'RE TINY, THEY'RE INVISIBLE AND THEY DON'T LIKE US VERY MUCH.
WELL I DON'T LIKE THEM!
Dear to whom it may concern,
Please Leave us alone!
We are nice People Please stop being mean.
All the best, Hilda xx
LISTEN UP LITTLE GUYS! THIS ONE'S FOR YOU!

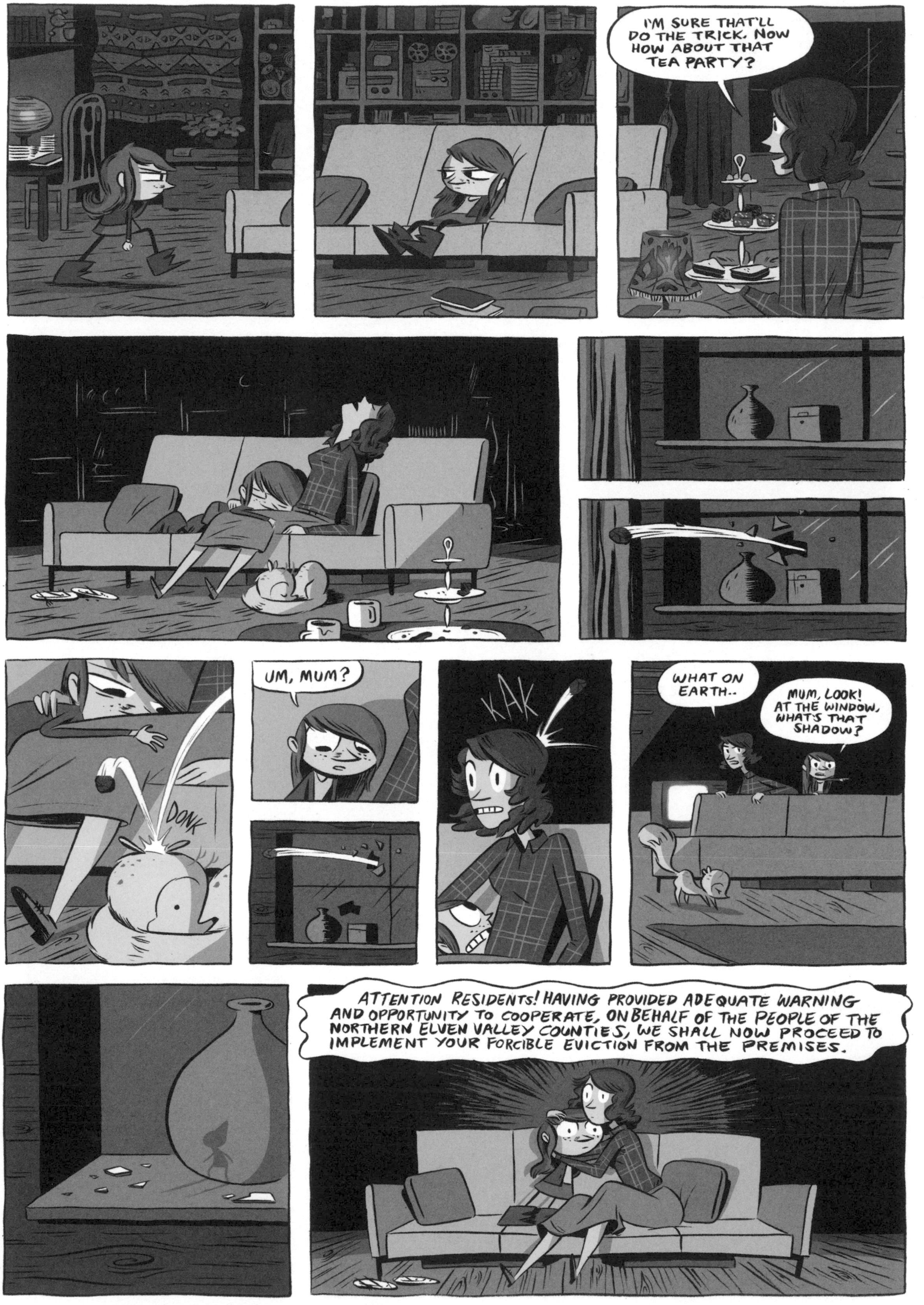
I'M SURE THAT'LL DO THE TRICK. NOW HOW ABOUT THAT TEA PARTY?
DONK
UM, MUM?
KAK
WHAT ON EARTH..
MUM, LOOK! AT THE WINDOW. WHAT'S THAT SHADOW?
ATTENTION RESIDENTS! HAVING PROVIDED ADEQUATE WARNING AND OPPORTUNITY TO COOPERATE, ON BEHALF OF THE PEOPLE OF THE NORTHERN ELVEN VALLEY COUNTIES, WE SHALL NOW PROCEED TO IMPLEMENT YOUR FORCIBLE EVICTION FROM THE PREMISES.

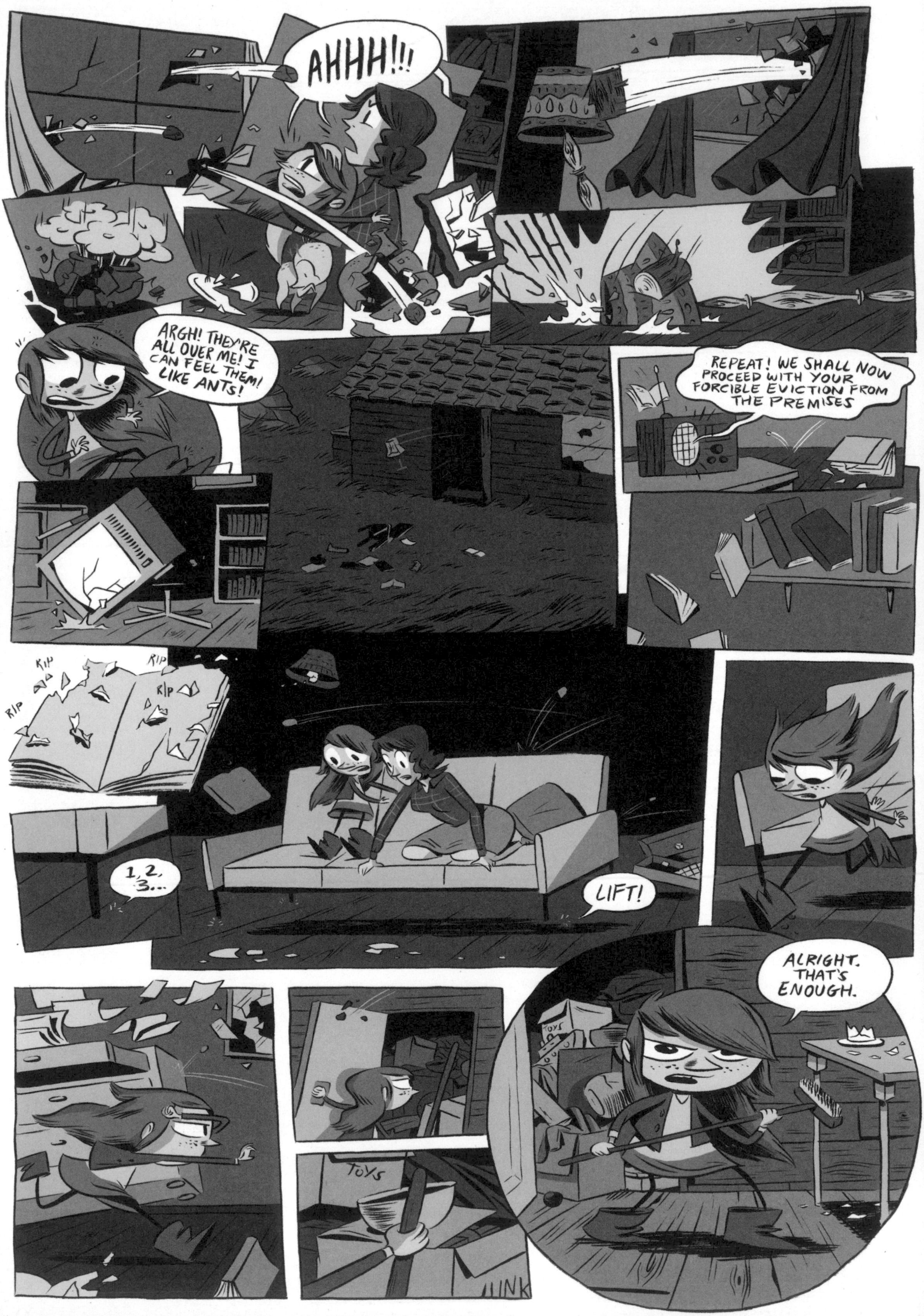
AHHH!!!
ARGH! THEY'RE ALL OVER ME! I CAN FEEL THEM! LIKE ANTS!
REPEAT! WE SHALL NOW PROCEED WITH YOUR FORCIBLE EVICTION FROM THE PREMISES
RIP
RIP
RIP
RIP
1, 2, 3...
LIFT!
TOYS
TOYS
ALRIGHT. THAT'S ENOUGH.
JUNK

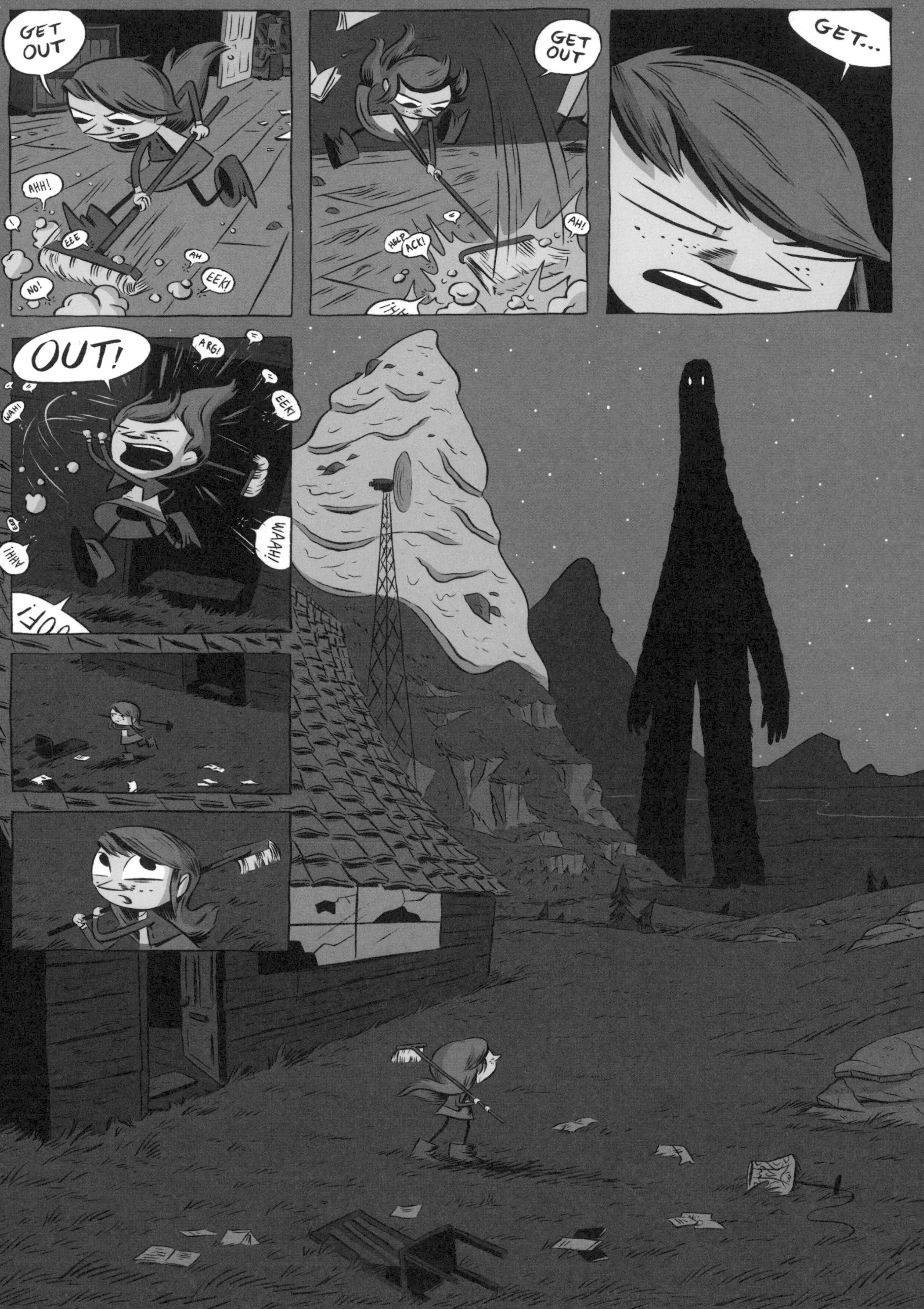
GET OUT
AHH!
!
EEE
AH
EEK!
NO!
GET OUT
HELP
ACK!
AH!
GET...
OUT!
ARG!
WAH!
EEK!
WAAH!
AHH!

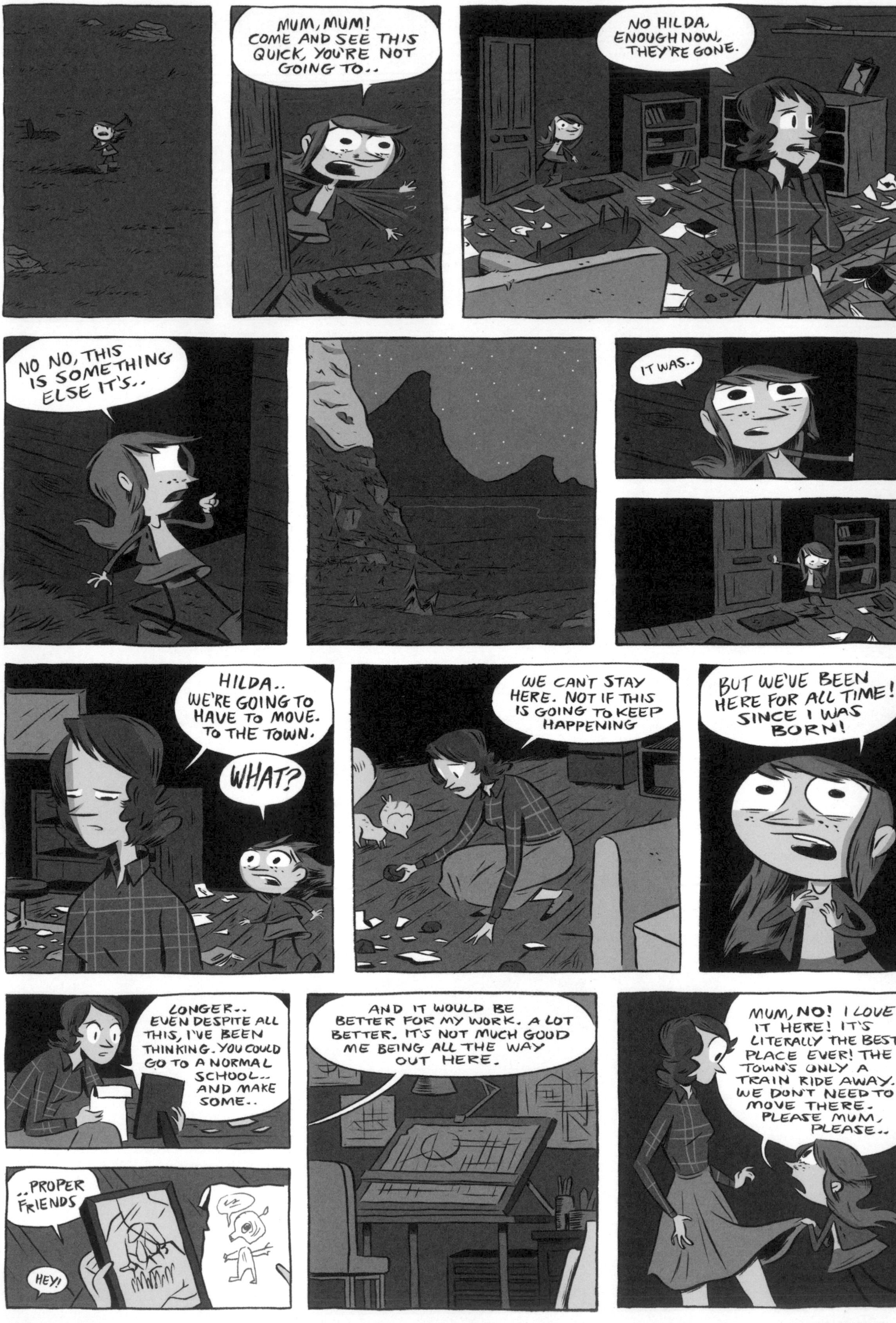
MUM, MUM! COME AND SEE THIS QUICK, YOU'RE NOT GOING TO..
NO HILDA, ENOUGH NOW, THEY'RE GONE.
NO NO, THIS IS SOMETHING ELSE IT'S..
IT WAS..
HILDA.. WE'RE GOING TO HAVE TO MOVE. TO THE TOWN.
WHAT?
WE CAN'T STAY HERE. NOT IF THIS IS GOING TO KEEP HAPPENING
BUT WE'VE BEEN HERE FOR ALL TIME! SINCE I WAS BORN!
LONGER.. EVEN DESPITE ALL THIS, I'VE BEEN THINKING. YOU COULD GO TO A NORMAL SCHOOL.. AND MAKE SOME..
..PROPER FRIENDS
HEY!
AND IT WOULD BE BETTER FOR MY WORK. A LOT BETTER. IT'S NOT MUCH GOOD ME BEING ALL THE WAY OUT HERE.
MUM, NO! I LOVE IT HERE! IT'S LITERALLY THE BEST PLACE EVER! THE TOWN'S ONLY A TRAIN RIDE AWAY. WE DON'T NEED TO MOVE THERE. PLEASE MUM, PLEASE..

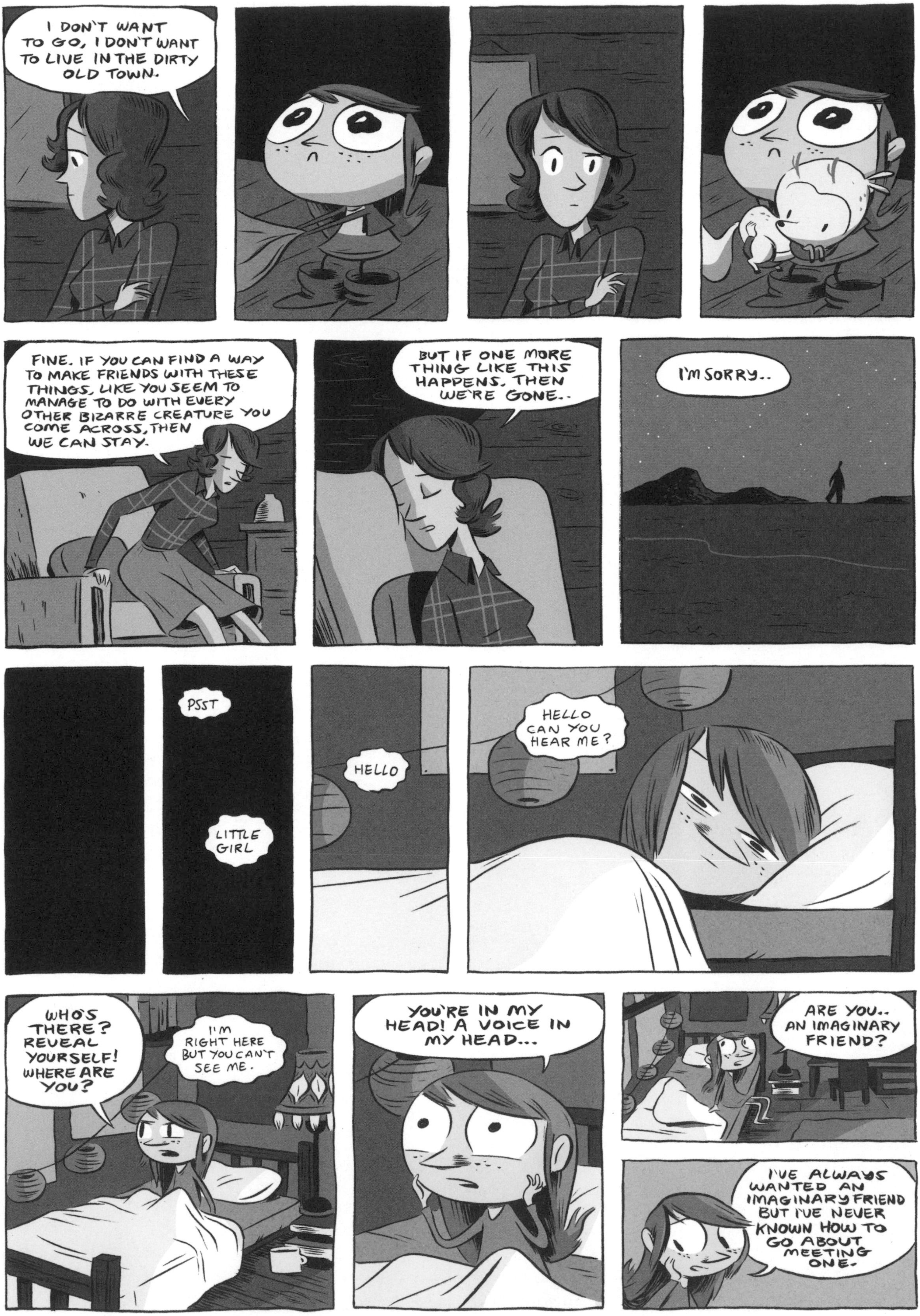
I DON'T WANT TO GO, I DON'T WANT TO LIVE IN THE DIRTY OLD TOWN.
FINE. IF YOU CAN FIND A WAY TO MAKE FRIENDS WITH THESE THINGS, LIKE YOU SEEM TO MANAGE TO DO WITH EVERY OTHER BIZARRE CREATURE YOU COME ACROSS, THEN WE CAN STAY.
BUT IF ONE MORE THING LIKE THIS HAPPENS. THEN WE'RE GONE..
I'M SORRY..
PSST
LITTLE GIRL
HELLO
HELLO CAN YOU HEAR ME?
WHO'S THERE? REVEAL YOURSELF! WHERE ARE YOU?
I'M RIGHT HERE BUT YOU CAN'T SEE ME.
YOU'RE IN MY HEAD! A VOICE IN MY HEAD...
ARE YOU.. AN IMAGINARY FRIEND?
I'VE ALWAYS WANTED AN IMAGINARY FRIEND BUT I'VE NEVER KNOWN HOW TO GO ABOUT MEETING ONE.

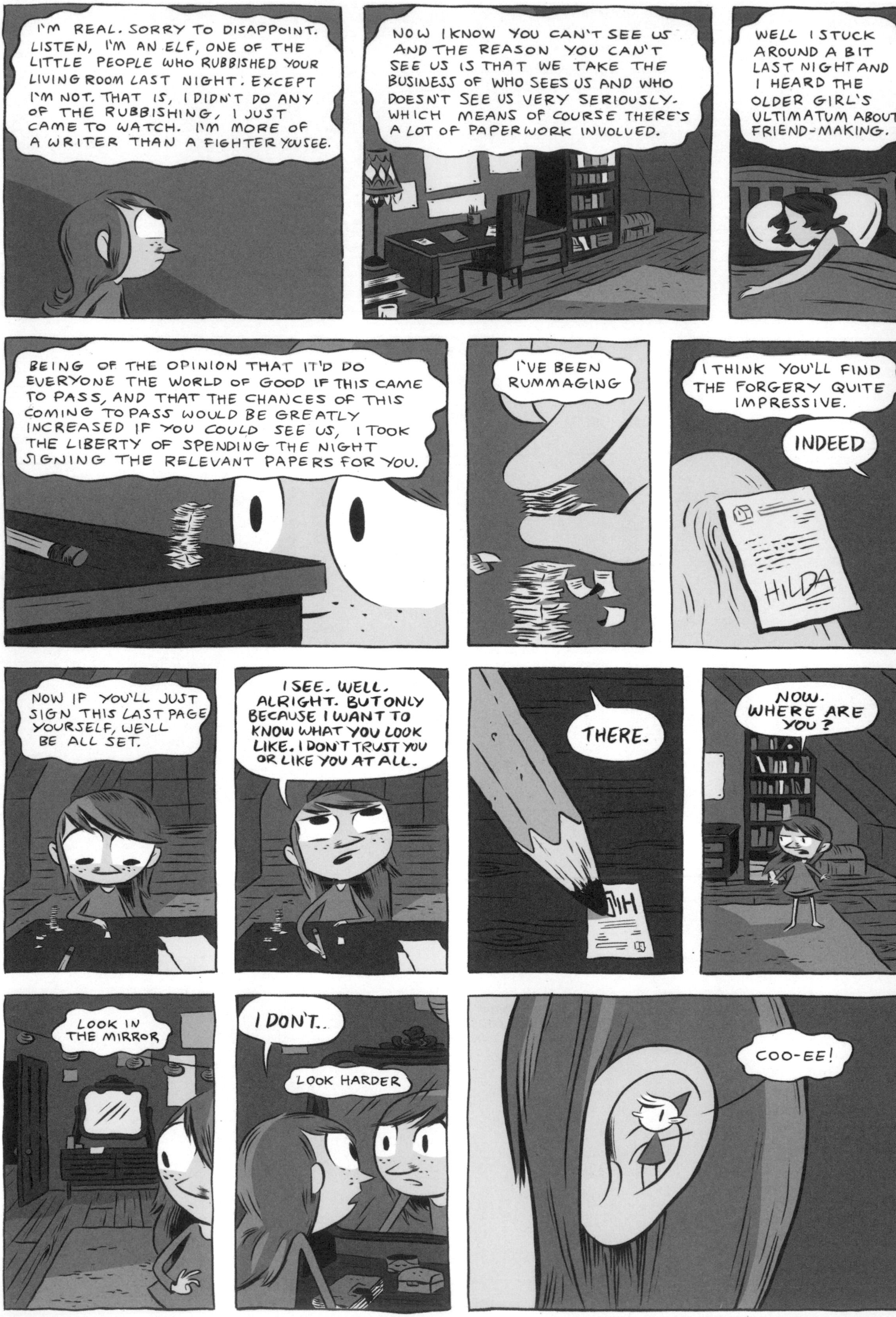
I'M REAL. SORRY TO DISAPPOINT. LISTEN, I'M AN ELF, ONE OF THE LITTLE PEOPLE WHO RUBBISHED YOUR LIVING ROOM LAST NIGHT. EXCEPT I'M NOT. THAT IS, I DIDN'T DO ANY OF THE RUBBISHING, I JUST CAME TO WATCH. I'M MORE OF A WRITER THAN A FIGHTER YOU SEE.
NOW I KNOW YOU CAN'T SEE US AND THE REASON YOU CAN'T SEE US IS THAT WE TAKE THE BUSINESS OF WHO SEES US AND WHO DOESN'T SEE US VERY SERIOUSLY. WHICH MEANS OF COURSE THERE'S A LOT OF PAPERWORK INVOLVED.
WELL I STUCK AROUND A BIT LAST NIGHT AND I HEARD THE OLDER GIRL'S ULTIMATUM ABOUT FRIEND-MAKING.
BEING OF THE OPINION THAT IT'D DO EVERYONE THE WORLD OF GOOD IF THIS CAME TO PASS, AND THAT THE CHANCES OF THIS COMING TO PASS WOULD BE GREATLY INCREASED IF YOU COULD SEE US, I TOOK THE LIBERTY OF SPENDING THE NIGHT SIGNING THE RELEVANT PAPERS FOR YOU.
I'VE BEEN RUMMAGING
I THINK YOU'LL FIND THE FORGERY QUITE IMPRESSIVE.
INDEED
HILDA
NOW IF YOU'LL JUST SIGN THIS LAST PAGE YOURSELF, WE'LL BE ALL SET.
I SEE. WELL. ALRIGHT. BUT ONLY BECAUSE I WANT TO KNOW WHAT YOU LOOK LIKE. I DON'T TRUST YOU OR LIKE YOU AT ALL.
THERE.
NOW. WHERE ARE YOU?
LOOK IN THE MIRROR
I DON'T..
LOOK HARDER
COO-EE!

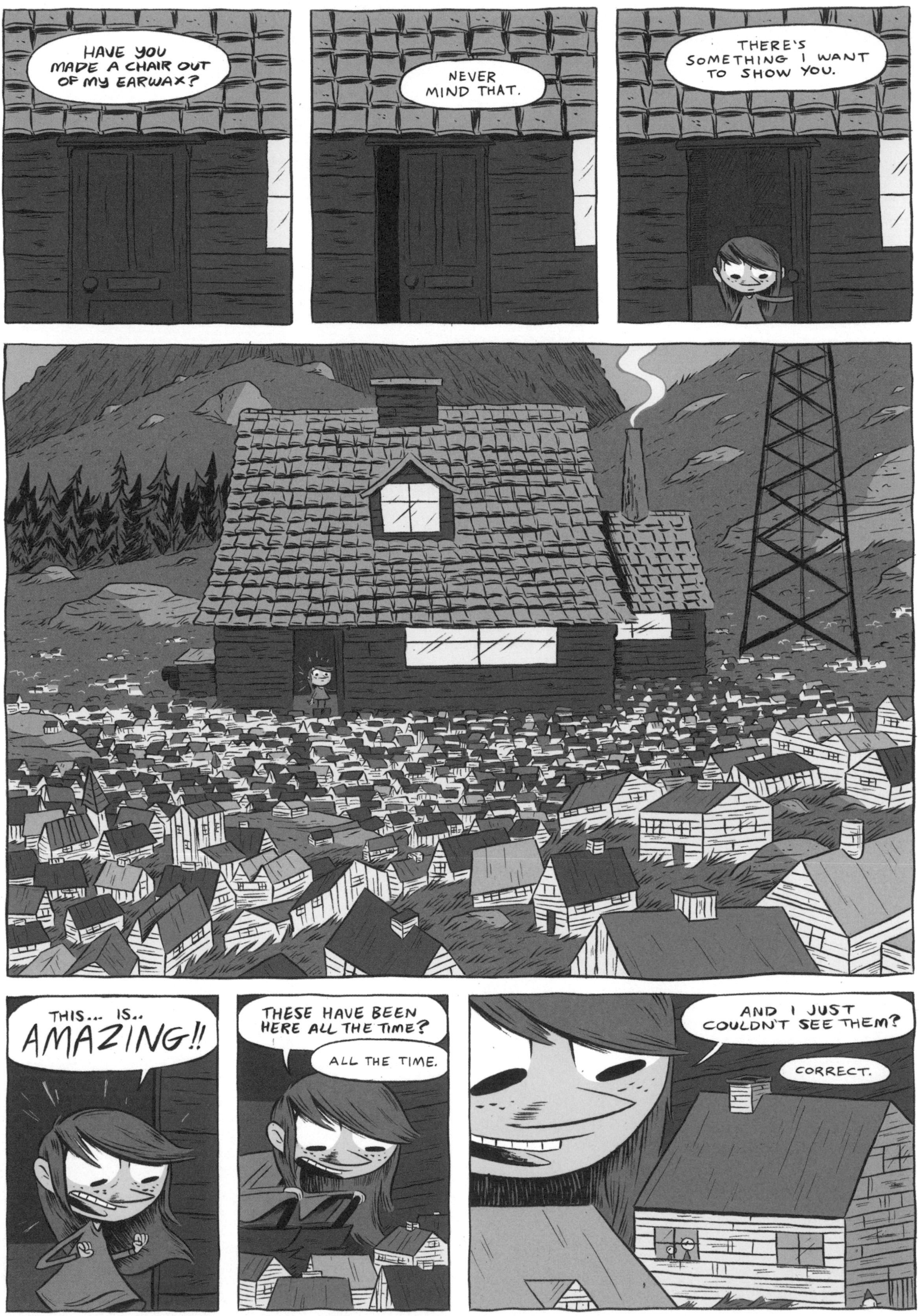
HAVE YOU MADE A CHAIR OUT OF MY EARWAX?
NEVER MIND THAT.
THERE'S SOMETHING I WANT TO SHOW YOU.
THIS... IS.. AMAZING!!
THESE HAVE BEEN HERE ALL THE TIME?
ALL THE TIME.
AND I JUST COULDN'T SEE THEM?
CORRECT.

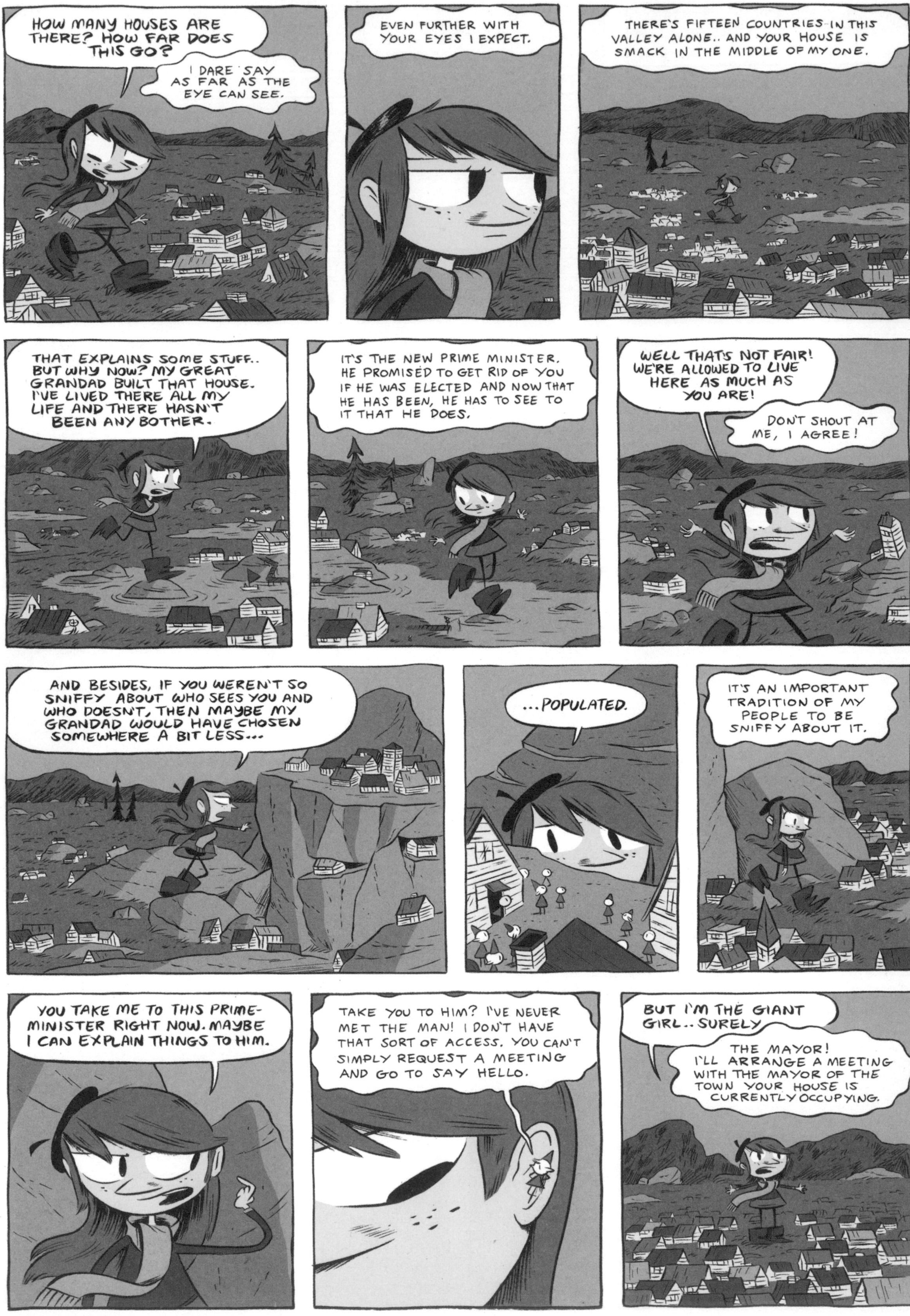
HOW MANY HOUSES ARE THERE? HOW FAR DOES THIS GO?
I DARE SAY AS FAR AS THE EYE CAN SEE.
EVEN FURTHER WITH YOUR EYES I EXPECT.
THERE'S FIFTEEN COUNTRIES IN THIS VALLEY ALONE.. AND YOUR HOUSE IS SMACK IN THE MIDDLE OF MY ONE.
THAT EXPLAINS SOME STUFF.. BUT WHY NOW? MY GREAT GRANDAD BUILT THAT HOUSE. I'VE LIVED THERE ALL MY LIFE AND THERE HASN'T BEEN ANY BOTHER.
IT'S THE NEW PRIME MINISTER. HE PROMISED TO GET RID OF YOU IF HE WAS ELECTED AND NOW THAT HE HAS BEEN, HE HAS TO SEE TO IT THAT HE DOES.
WELL THAT'S NOT FAIR! WE'RE ALLOWED TO LIVE HERE AS MUCH AS YOU ARE!
DON'T SHOUT AT ME, I AGREE!
AND BESIDES, IF YOU WEREN'T SO SNIFFY ABOUT WHO SEES YOU AND WHO DOESN'T, THEN MAYBE MY GRANDAD WOULD HAVE CHOSEN SOMEWHERE A BIT LESS...
...POPULATED.
IT'S AN IMPORTANT TRADITION OF MY PEOPLE TO BE SNIFFY ABOUT IT.
YOU TAKE ME TO THIS PRIME-MINISTER RIGHT NOW. MAYBE I CAN EXPLAIN THINGS TO HIM.
TAKE YOU TO HIM? I'VE NEVER MET THE MAN! I DON'T HAVE THAT SORT OF ACCESS. YOU CAN'T SIMPLY REQUEST A MEETING AND GO TO SAY HELLO.
BUT I'M THE GIANT GIRL.. SURELY
THE MAYOR! I'LL ARRANGE A MEETING WITH THE MAYOR OF THE TOWN YOUR HOUSE IS CURRENTLY OCCUPYING.

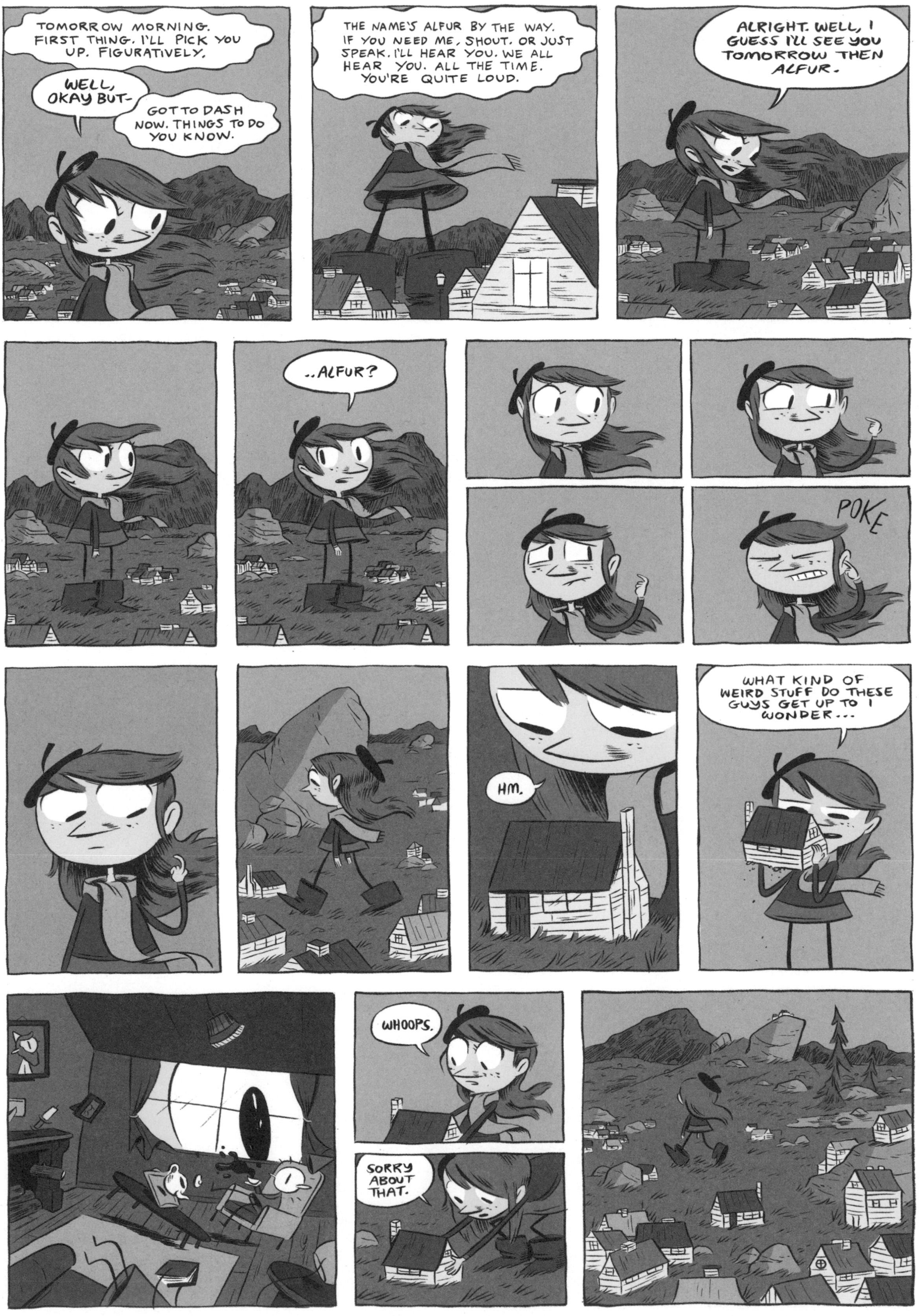
TOMORROW MORNING. FIRST THING. I'LL PICK YOU UP. FIGURATIVELY.
WELL, OKAY BUT-
GOT TO DASH NOW. THINGS TO DO YOU KNOW.
THE NAME'S ALFUR BY THE WAY. IF YOU NEED ME, SHOUT. OR JUST SPEAK. I'LL HEAR YOU. WE ALL HEAR YOU. ALL THE TIME. YOU'RE QUITE LOUD.
ALRIGHT. WELL, I GUESS I'LL SEE YOU TOMORROW THEN ALFUR.
..ALFUR?
POKE
HM.
WHAT KIND OF WEIRD STUFF DO THESE GUYS GET UP TO I WONDER...
WHOOPS.
SORRY ABOUT THAT.

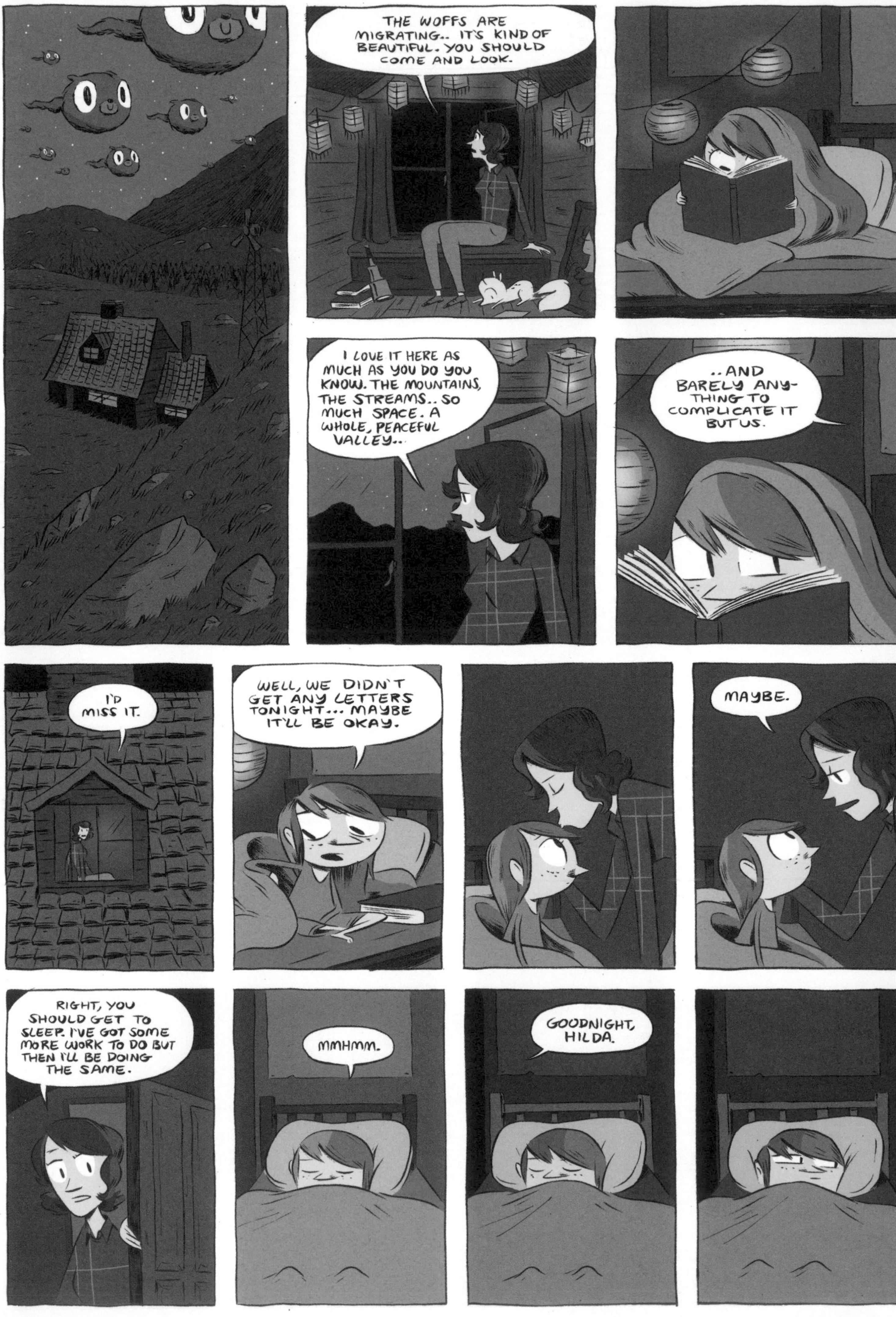
THE WOFFS ARE MIGRATING.. IT'S KIND OF BEAUTIFUL. YOU SHOULD COME AND LOOK.
I LOVE IT HERE AS MUCH AS YOU DO YOU KNOW. THE MOUNTAINS, THE STREAMS.. SO MUCH SPACE. A WHOLE, PEACEFUL VALLEY..
..AND BARELY ANYTHING TO COMPLICATE IT BUT US.
I'D MISS IT.
WELL, WE DIDN'T GET ANY LETTERS TONIGHT... MAYBE IT'LL BE OKAY.
MAYBE.
RIGHT, YOU SHOULD GET TO SLEEP. I'VE GOT SOME MORE WORK TO DO BUT THEN I'LL BE DOING THE SAME.
MMHMM.
GOODNIGHT, HILDA.

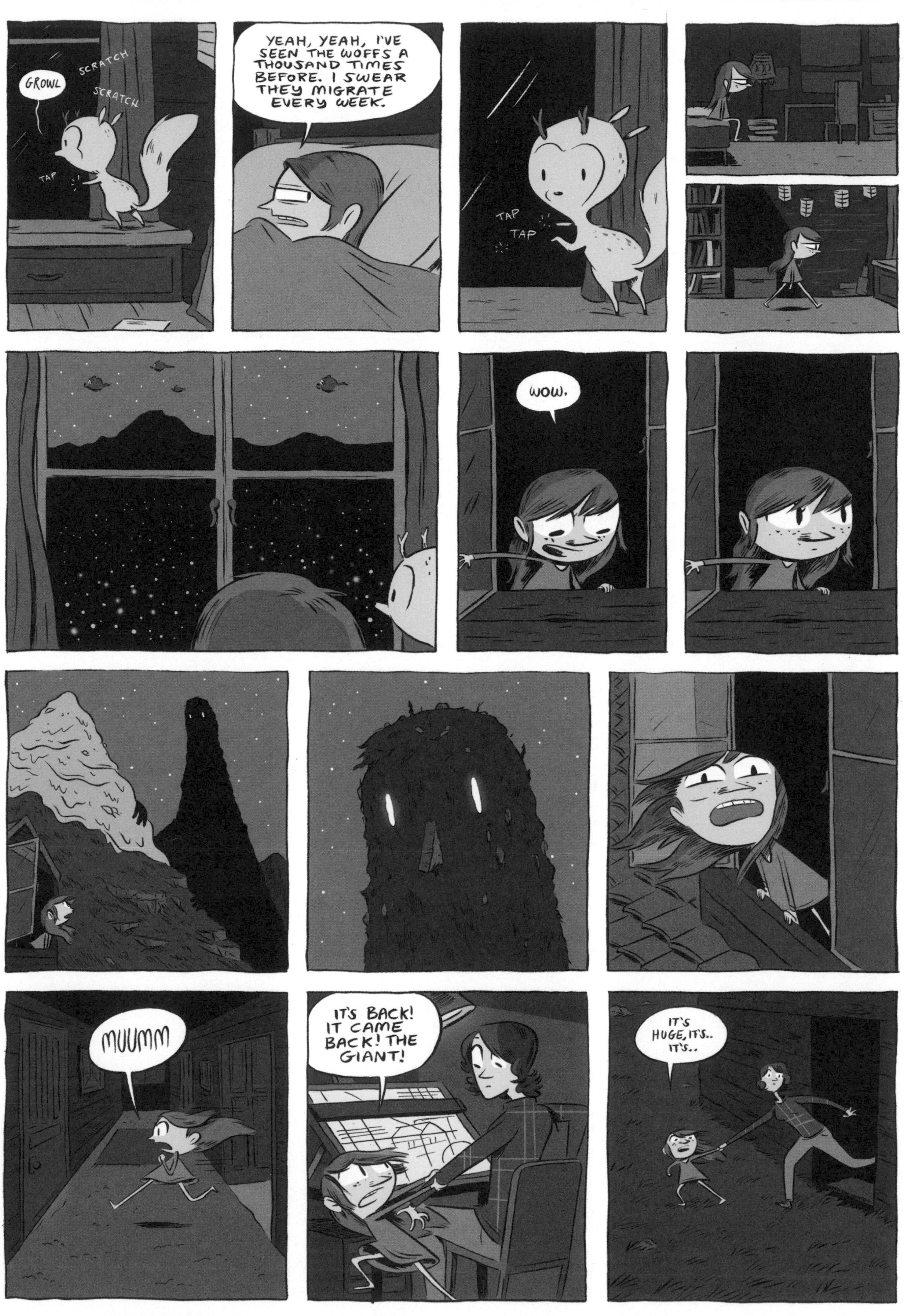
GROWL
SCRATCH
SCRATCH
TAP
YEAH, YEAH, I'VE SEEN THE WOFFS A THOUSAND TIMES BEFORE. I SWEAR THEY MIGRATE EVERY WEEK.
TAP
TAP
WOW.
MUUMM
IT'S BACK! IT CAME BACK! THE GIANT!
IT'S HUGE, IT'S.. IT'S..

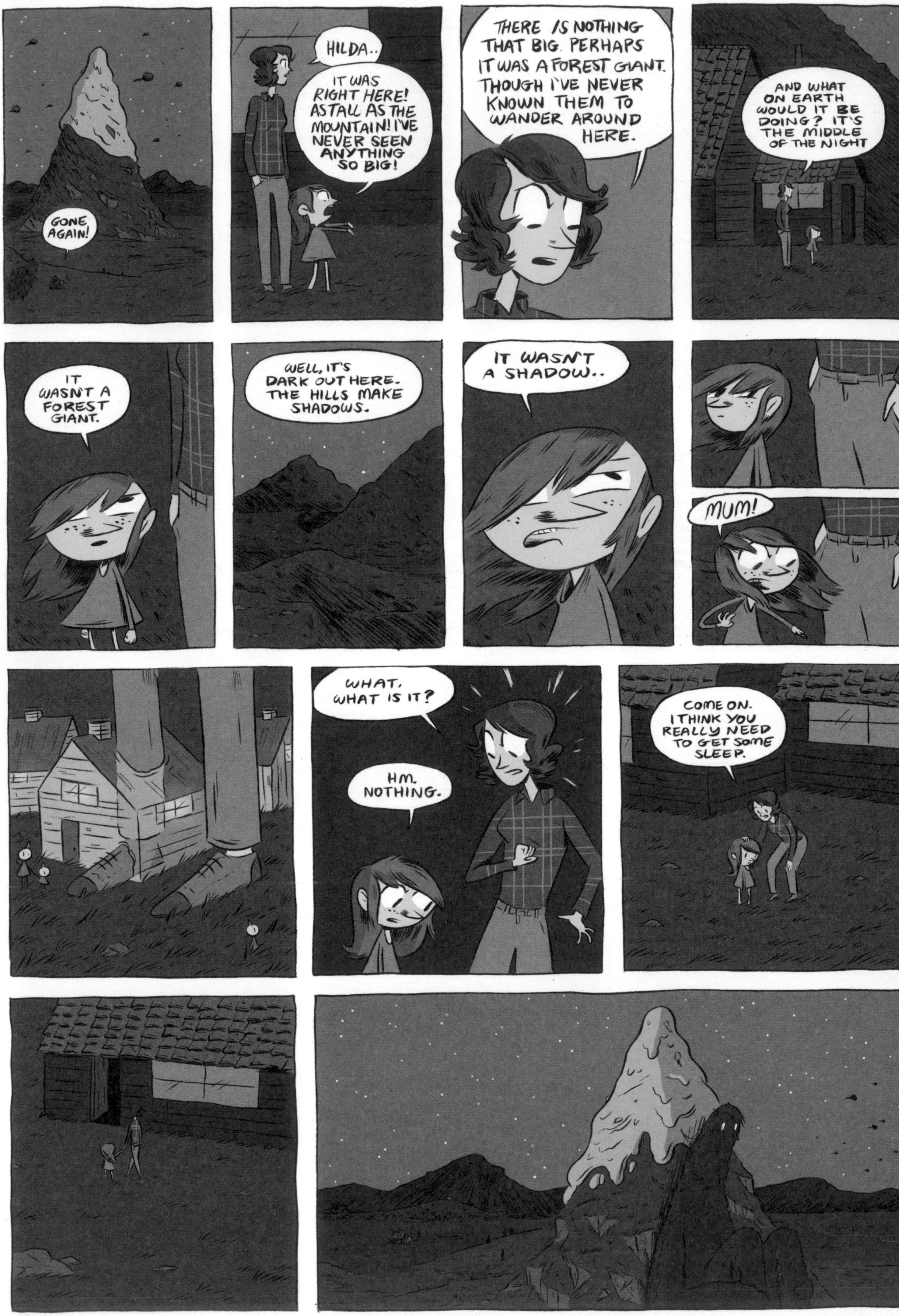
GONE AGAIN!
HILDA..
IT WAS RIGHT HERE! AS TALL AS THE MOUNTAIN! I'VE NEVER SEEN ANYTHING SO BIG!
THERE IS NOTHING THAT BIG. PERHAPS IT WAS A FOREST GIANT. THOUGH I'VE NEVER KNOWN THEM TO WANDER AROUND HERE.
AND WHAT ON EARTH WOULD IT BE DOING? IT'S THE MIDDLE OF THE NIGHT
IT WASN'T A FOREST GIANT.
WELL, IT'S DARK OUT HERE. THE HILLS MAKE SHADOWS.
IT WASN'T A SHADOW..
MUM!
WHAT, WHAT IS IT?
HM. NOTHING.
COME ON. I THINK YOU REALLY NEED TO GET SOME SLEEP.

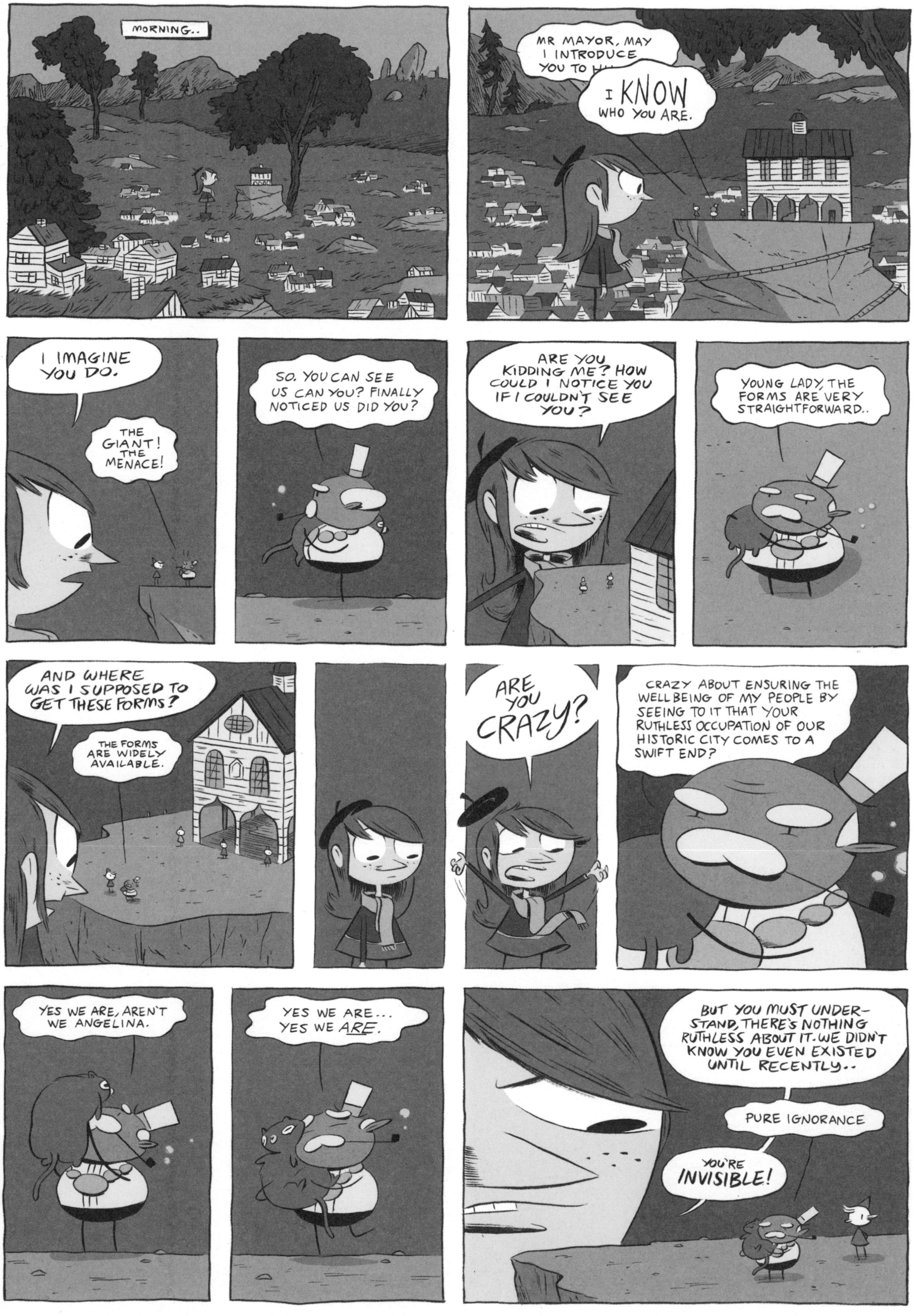
MORNING..
MR MAYOR, MAY I INTRODUCE YOU TO
I KNOW WHO YOU ARE.
I IMAGINE YOU DO.
THE GIANT! THE MENACE!
SO. YOU CAN SEE US CAN YOU? FINALLY NOTICED US DID YOU?
ARE YOU KIDDING ME? HOW COULD I NOTICE YOU IF I COULDN'T SEE YOU?
YOUNG LADY, THE FORMS ARE VERY STRAIGHTFORWARD..
AND WHERE WAS I SUPPOSED TO GET THESE FORMS?
THE FORMS ARE WIDELY AVAILABLE.
ARE YOU CRAZY?
CRAZY ABOUT ENSURING THE WELL BEING OF MY PEOPLE BY SEEING TO IT THAT YOUR RUTHLESS OCCUPATION OF OUR HISTORIC CITY COMES TO A SWIFT END?
YES WE ARE, AREN'T WE ANGELINA.
YES WE ARE... YES WE ARE.
BUT YOU MUST UNDERSTAND, THERE'S NOTHING RUTHLESS ABOUT IT. WE DIDN'T KNOW YOU EVEN EXISTED UNTIL RECENTLY..
PURE IGNORANCE
YOU'RE INVISIBLE!

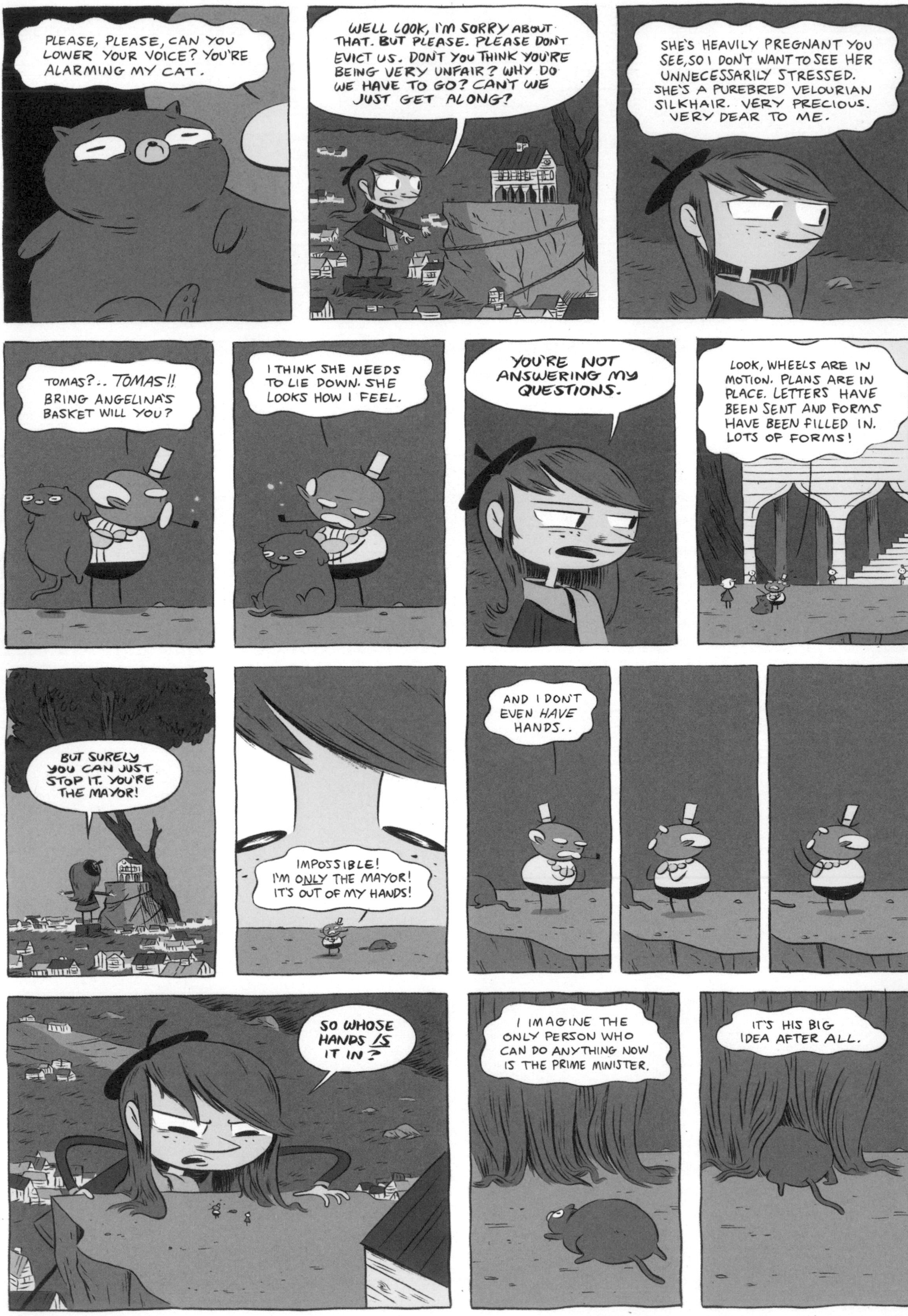
PLEASE, PLEASE, CAN YOU LOWER YOUR VOICE? YOU'RE ALARMING MY CAT.
WELL LOOK, I'M SORRY ABOUT THAT. BUT PLEASE. PLEASE DON'T EVICT US. DON'T YOU THINK YOU'RE BEING VERY UNFAIR? WHY DO WE HAVE TO GO? CAN'T WE JUST GET ALONG?
SHE'S HEAVILY PREGNANT YOU SEE, SO I DON'T WANT TO SEE HER UNNECESSARILY STRESSED. SHE'S A PUREBRED VELOURIAN SILKHAIR. VERY PRECIOUS. VERY DEAR TO ME.
TOMAS?.. TOMAS!! BRING ANGELINA'S BASKET WILL YOU?
I THINK SHE NEEDS TO LIE DOWN. SHE LOOKS HOW I FEEL.
YOU'RE NOT ANSWERING MY QUESTIONS.
LOOK, WHEELS ARE IN MOTION. PLANS ARE IN PLACE. LETTERS HAVE BEEN SENT AND FORMS HAVE BEEN FILLED IN. LOTS OF FORMS!
BUT SURELY YOU CAN JUST STOP IT. YOU'RE THE MAYOR!
IMPOSSIBLE! I'M ONLY THE MAYOR! IT'S OUT OF MY HANDS!
AND I DON'T EVEN HAVE HANDS..
SO WHOSE HANDS IS IT IN?
I IMAGINE THE ONLY PERSON WHO CAN DO ANYTHING NOW IS THE PRIME MINISTER.
IT'S HIS BIG IDEA AFTER ALL.

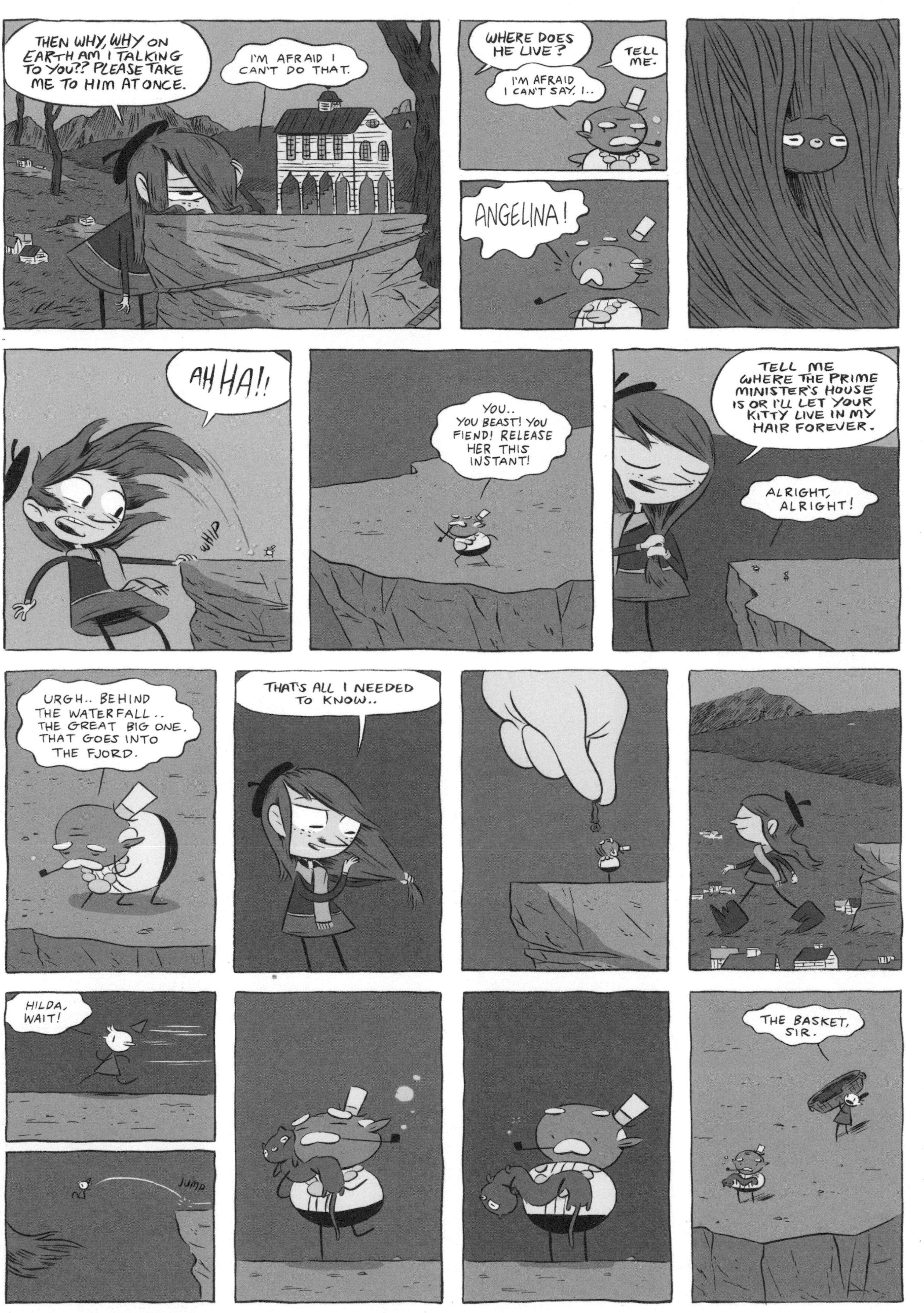
THEN WHY, WHY ON EARTH AM I TALKING TO YOU?? PLEASE TAKE ME TO HIM AT ONCE.
I'M AFRAID I CAN'T DO THAT.
WHERE DOES HE LIVE?
TELL ME.
I'M AFRAID I CAN'T SAY, I..
ANGELINA!
AH HA!!
WHIP
YOU.. YOU BEAST! YOU FIEND! RELEASE HER THIS INSTANT!
TELL ME WHERE THE PRIME MINISTER'S HOUSE IS OR I'LL LET YOUR KITTY LIVE IN MY HAIR FOREVER.
ALRIGHT, ALRIGHT!
URGH.. BEHIND THE WATERFALL.. THE GREAT BIG ONE. THAT GOES INTO THE FJORD.
THAT'S ALL I NEEDED TO KNOW..
HILDA, WAIT!
JUMP
THE BASKET, SIR.

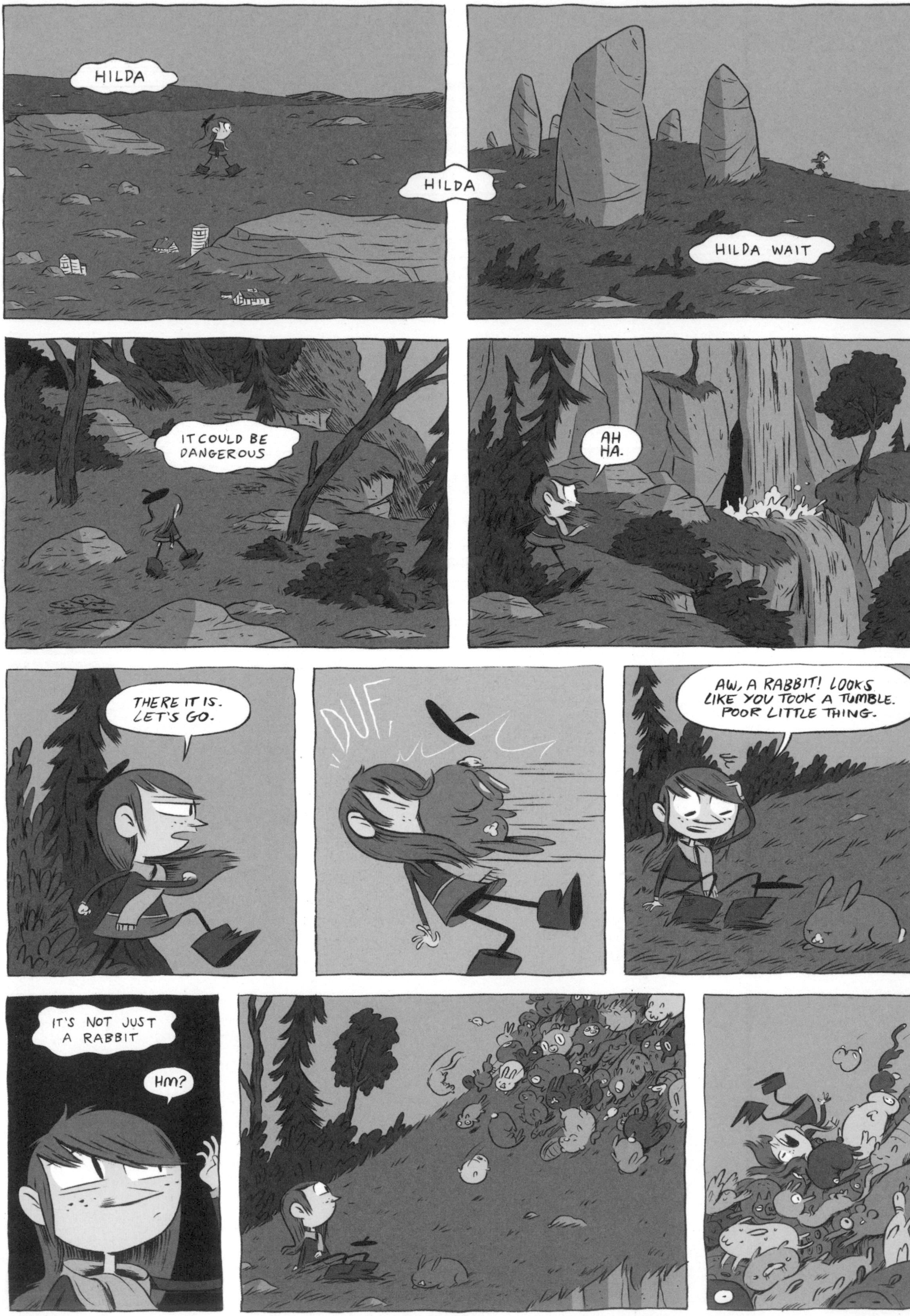
HILDA
HILDA
HILDA WAIT
IT COULD BE DANGEROUS
AH HA.
THERE IT IS. LET'S GO.
DUF,
AW, A RABBIT! LOOKS LIKE YOU TOOK A TUMBLE. POOR LITTLE THING.
IT'S NOT JUST A RABBIT
HM?

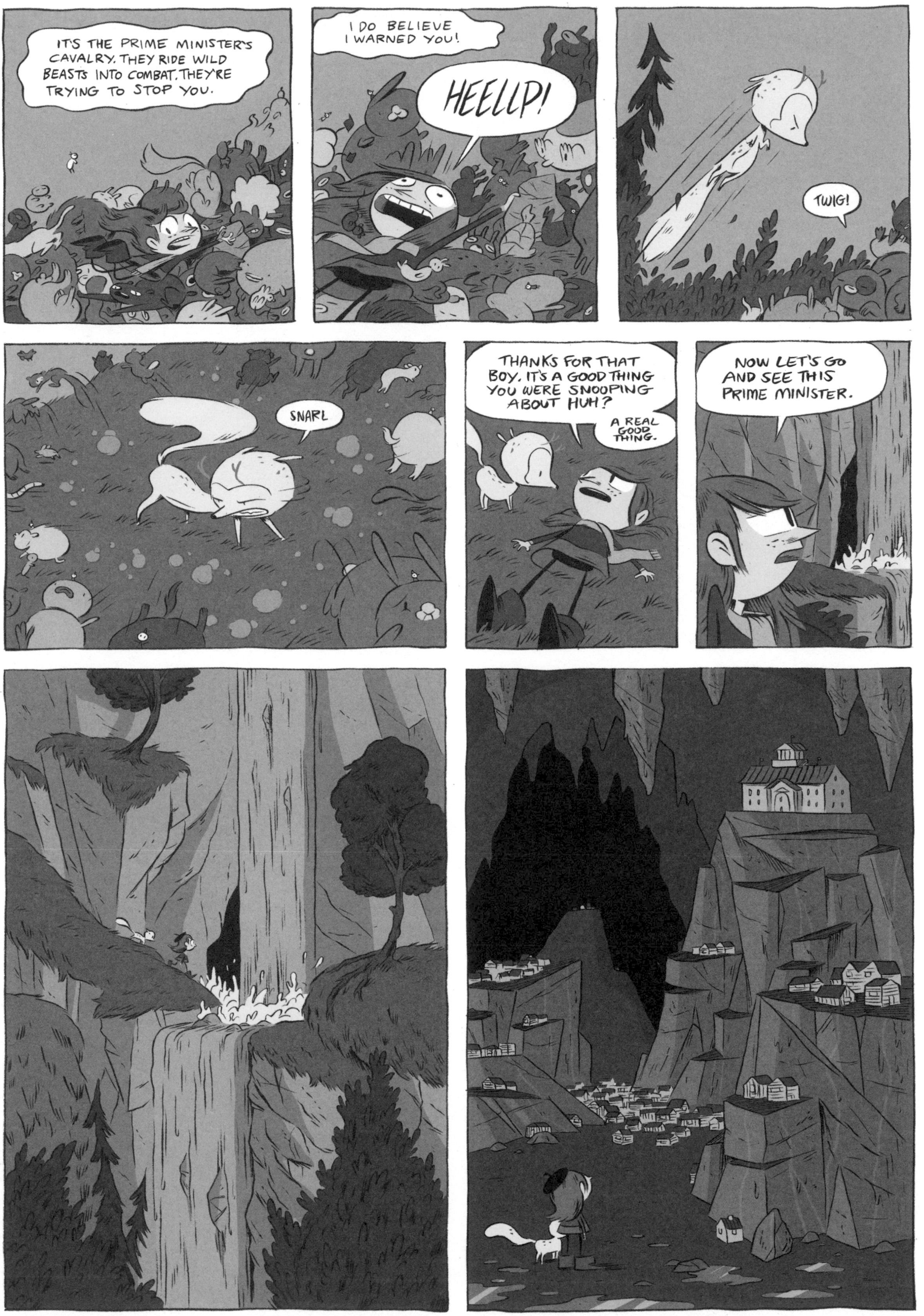
IT'S THE PRIME MINISTER'S CAVALRY. THEY RIDE WILD BEASTS INTO COMBAT. THEY'RE TRYING TO STOP YOU.
I DO BELIEVE I WARNED YOU!
HEELLP!
TWIG!
SNARL
THANKS FOR THAT BOY. IT'S A GOOD THING YOU WERE SNOOPING ABOUT HUH?
A REAL GOOD THING.
NOW LET'S GO AND SEE THIS PRIME MINISTER.

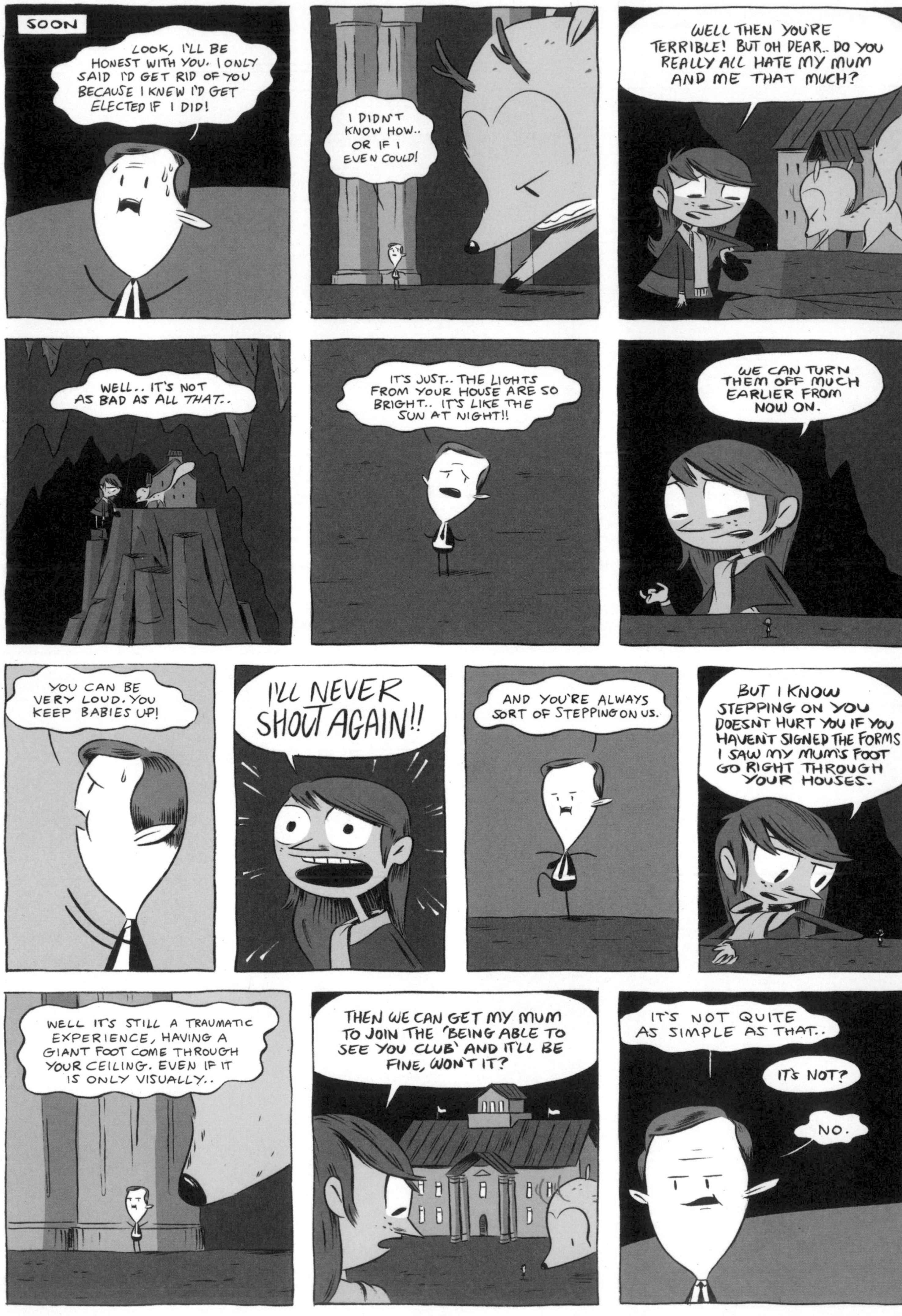
SOON
LOOK, I'LL BE HONEST WITH YOU. I ONLY SAID I'D GET RID OF YOU BECAUSE I KNEW I'D GET ELECTED IF I DID!
I DIDN'T KNOW HOW.. OR IF I EVEN COULD!
WELL THEN YOU'RE TERRIBLE! BUT OH DEAR.. DO YOU REALLY ALL HATE MY MUM AND ME THAT MUCH?
WELL.. IT'S NOT AS BAD AS ALL THAT..
IT'S JUST.. THE LIGHTS FROM YOUR HOUSE ARE SO BRIGHT.. IT'S LIKE THE SUN AT NIGHT!!
WE CAN TURN THEM OFF MUCH EARLIER FROM NOW ON.
YOU CAN BE VERY LOUD. YOU KEEP BABIES UP!
I'LL NEVER SHOUT AGAIN!!
AND YOU'RE ALWAYS SORT OF STEPPING ON US.
BUT I KNOW STEPPING ON YOU DOESN'T HURT YOU IF YOU HAVEN'T SIGNED THE FORMS I SAW MY MUM'S FOOT GO RIGHT THROUGH YOUR HOUSES.
WELL IT'S STILL A TRAUMATIC EXPERIENCE, HAVING A GIANT FOOT COME THROUGH YOUR CEILING. EVEN IF IT IS ONLY VISUALLY..
THEN WE CAN GET MY MUM TO JOIN THE 'BEING ABLE TO SEE YOU CLUB' AND IT'LL BE FINE, WON'T IT?
IT'S NOT QUITE AS SIMPLE AS THAT..
IT'S NOT?
NO.

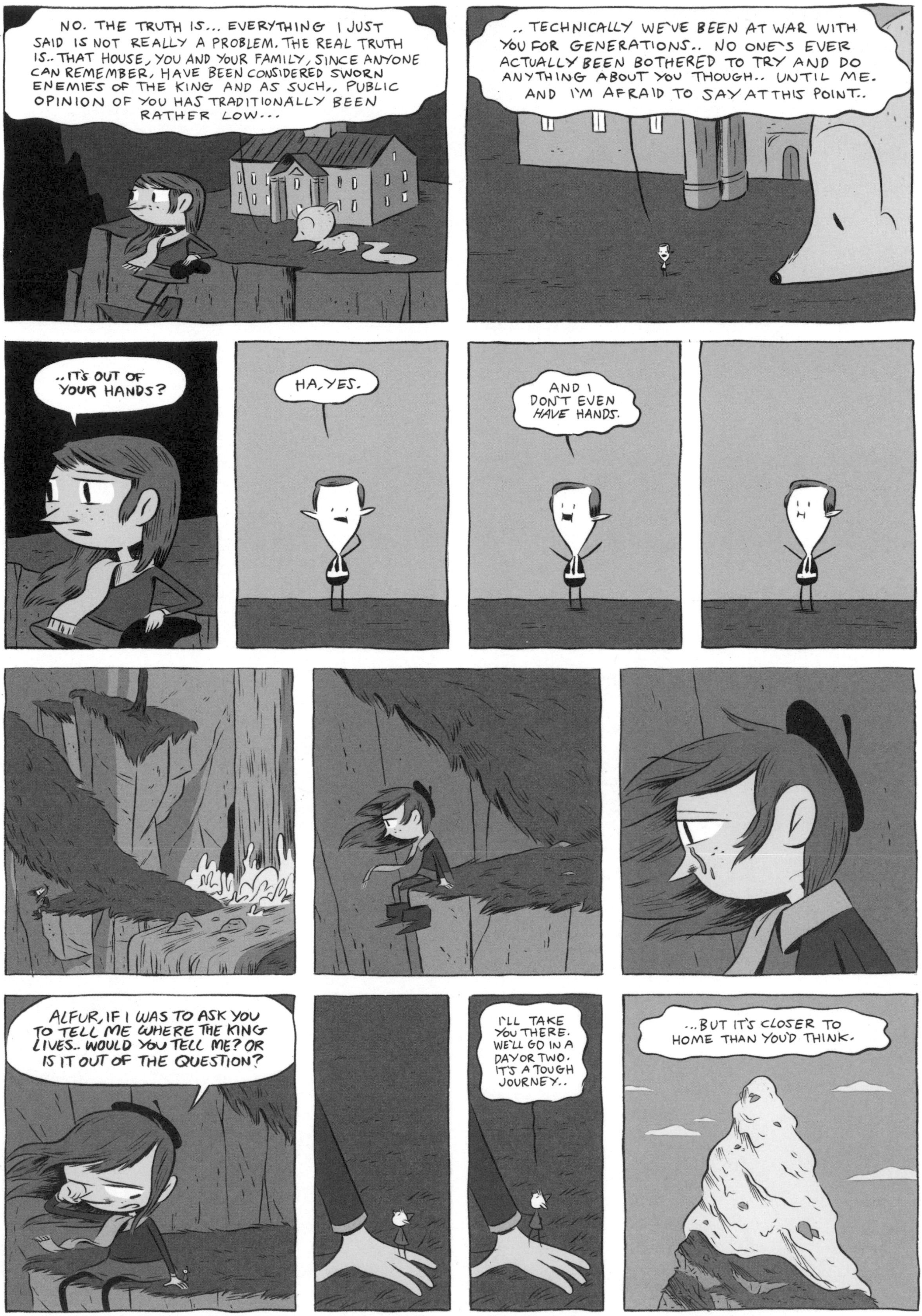
NO. THE TRUTH IS... EVERYTHING I JUST SAID IS NOT REALLY A PROBLEM. THE REAL TRUTH IS.. THAT HOUSE, YOU AND YOUR FAMILY, SINCE ANYONE CAN REMEMBER, HAVE BEEN CONSIDERED SWORN ENEMIES OF THE KING AND AS SUCH,, PUBLIC OPINION OF YOU HAS TRADITIONALLY BEEN RATHER LOW...
.. TECHNICALLY WE'VE BEEN AT WAR WITH YOU FOR GENERATIONS.. NO ONE'S EVER ACTUALLY BEEN BOTHERED TO TRY AND DO ANYTHING ABOUT YOU THOUGH.. UNTIL ME. AND I'M AFRAID TO SAY AT THIS POINT..
..IT'S OUT OF YOUR HANDS?
HA, YES.
AND I DON'T EVEN *HAVE* HANDS.
ALFUR, IF I WAS TO ASK YOU TO TELL ME WHERE THE KING LIVES.. WOULD YOU TELL ME? OR IS IT OUT OF THE QUESTION?
I'LL TAKE YOU THERE. WE'LL GO IN A DAY OR TWO. IT'S A TOUGH JOURNEY..
...BUT IT'S CLOSER TO HOME THAN YOU'D THINK.

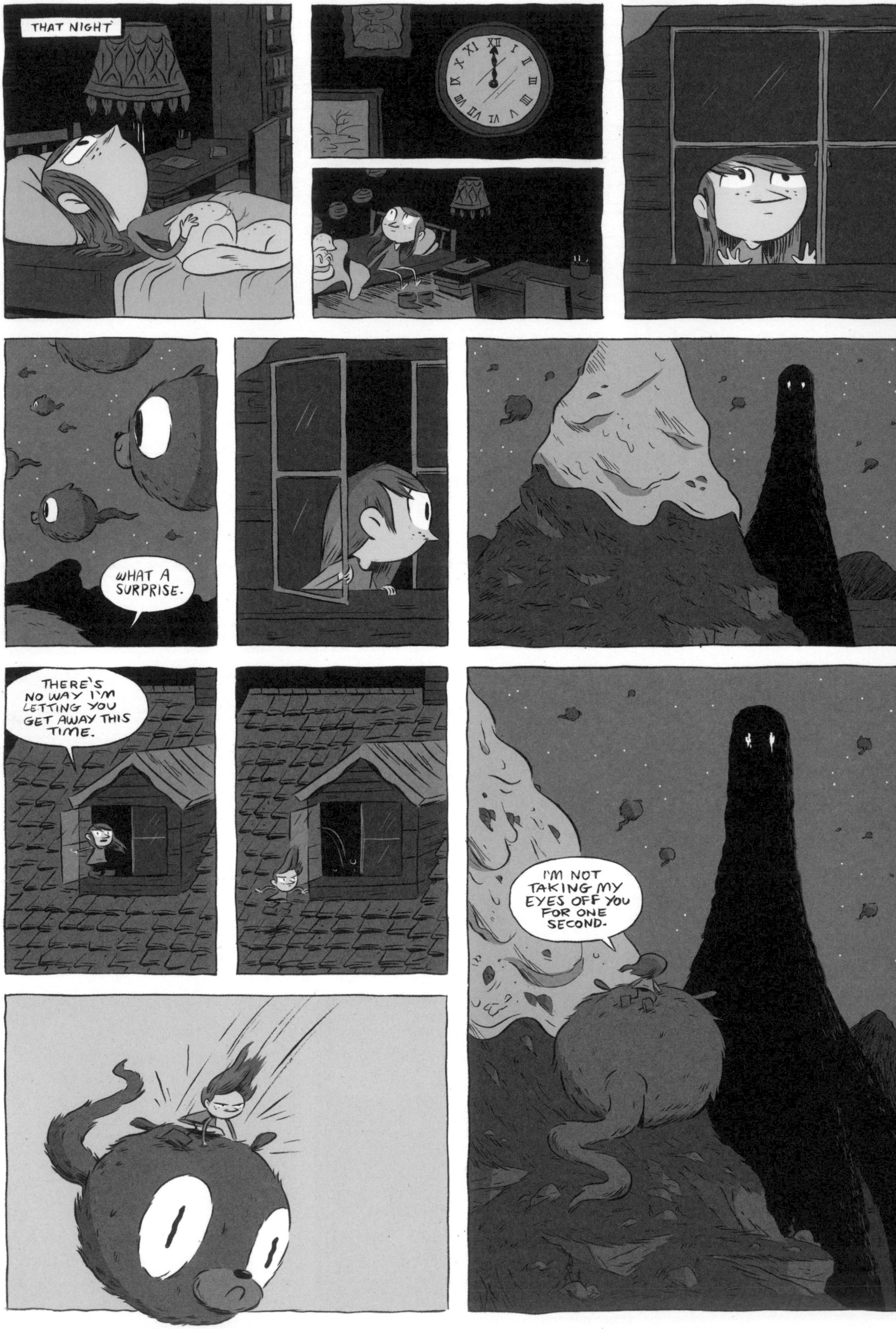
THAT NIGHT
WHAT A SURPRISE.
THERE'S NO WAY I'M LETTING YOU GET AWAY THIS TIME.
I'M NOT TAKING MY EYES OFF YOU FOR ONE SECOND.

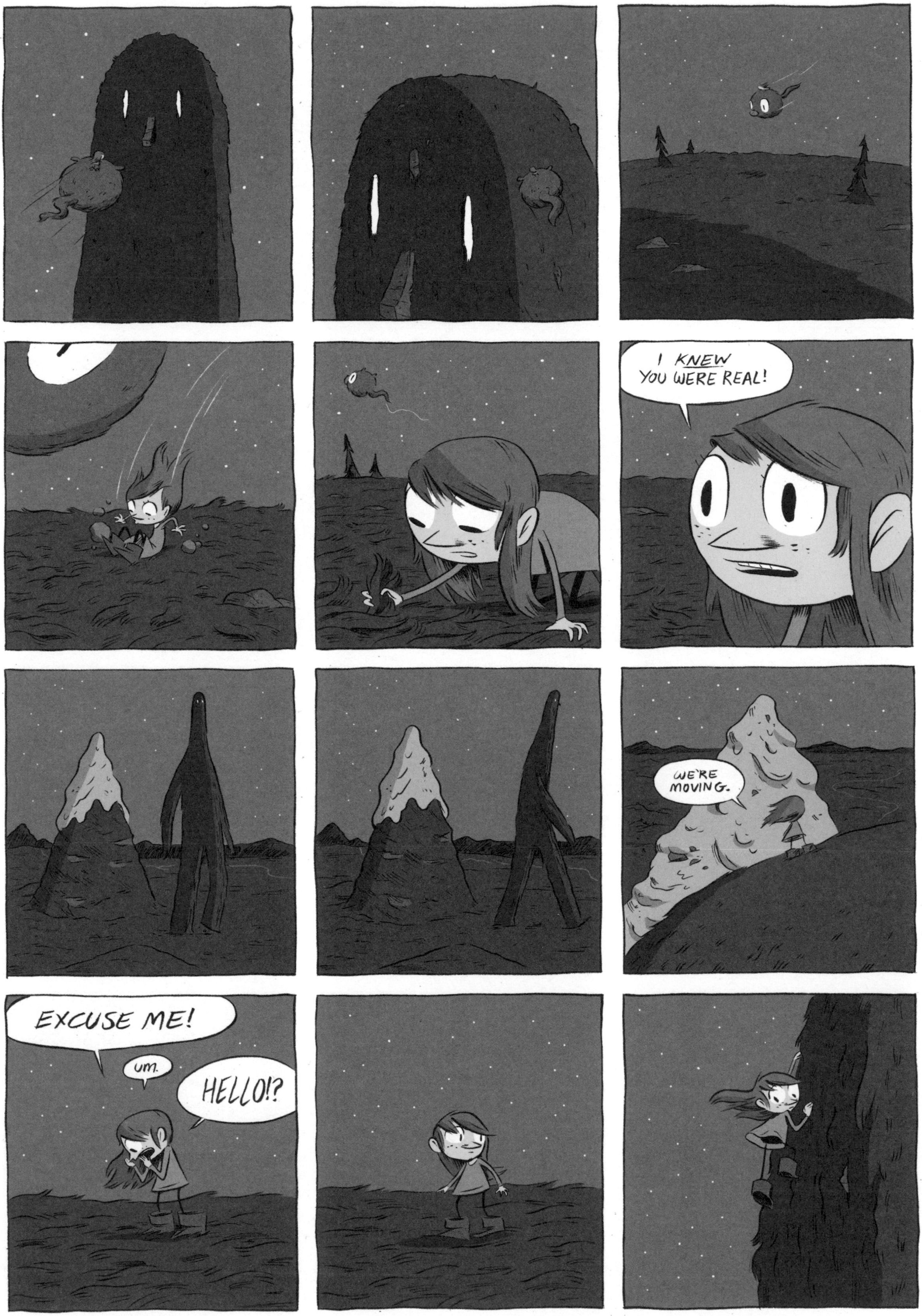

I KNEW YOU WERE REAL!
WE'RE MOVING.
EXCUSE ME!
um.
HELLO!?

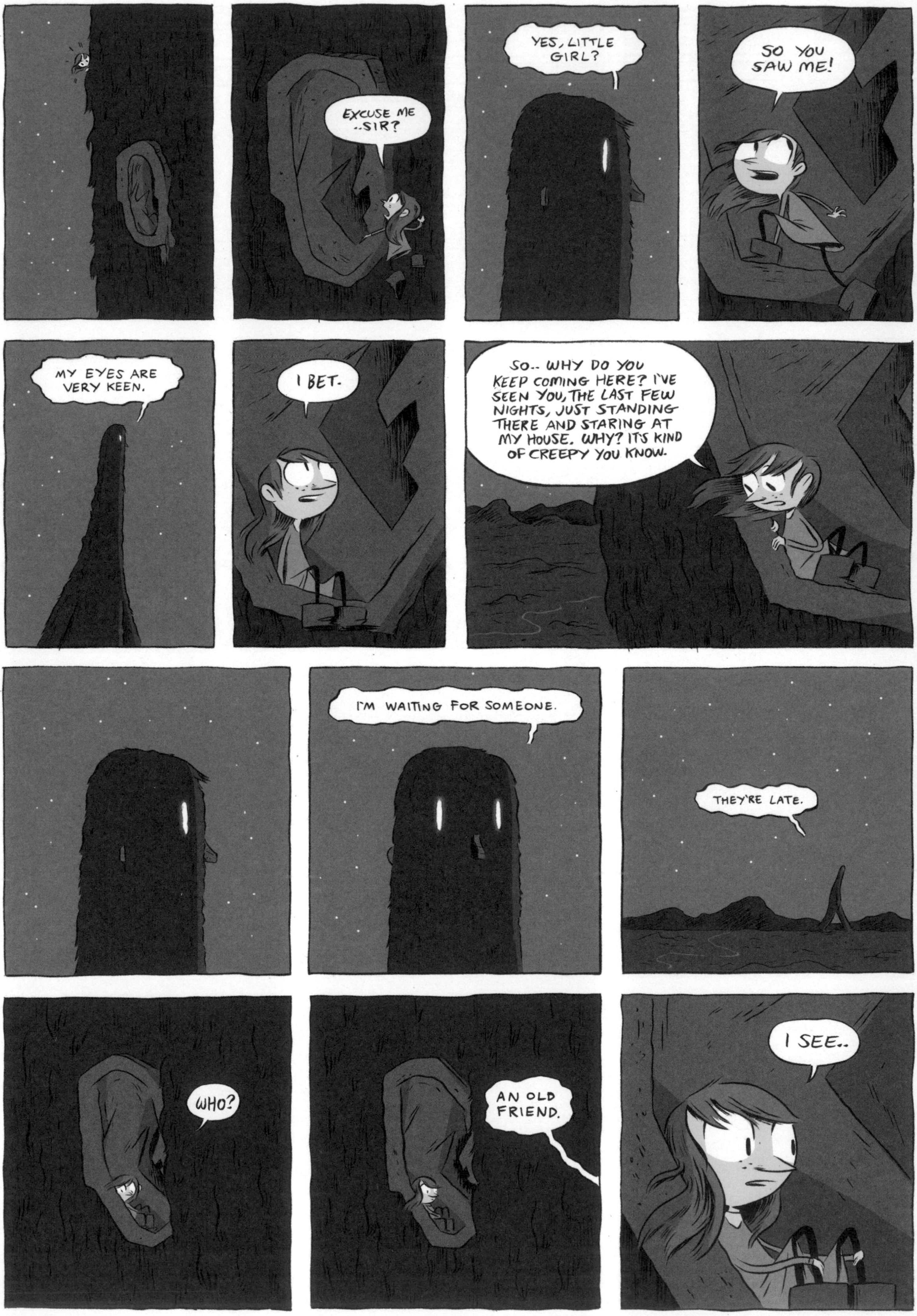
EXCUSE ME
..SIR?
YES, LITTLE
GIRL?
SO YOU
SAW ME!
MY EYES ARE
VERY KEEN.
I BET.
SO.. WHY DO YOU KEEP COMING HERE? I'VE SEEN YOU, THE LAST FEW NIGHTS, JUST STANDING THERE AND STARING AT MY HOUSE. WHY? IT'S KIND OF CREEPY YOU KNOW.
I'M WAITING FOR SOMEONE.
THEY'RE LATE.
WHO?
AN OLD
FRIEND.
I SEE..

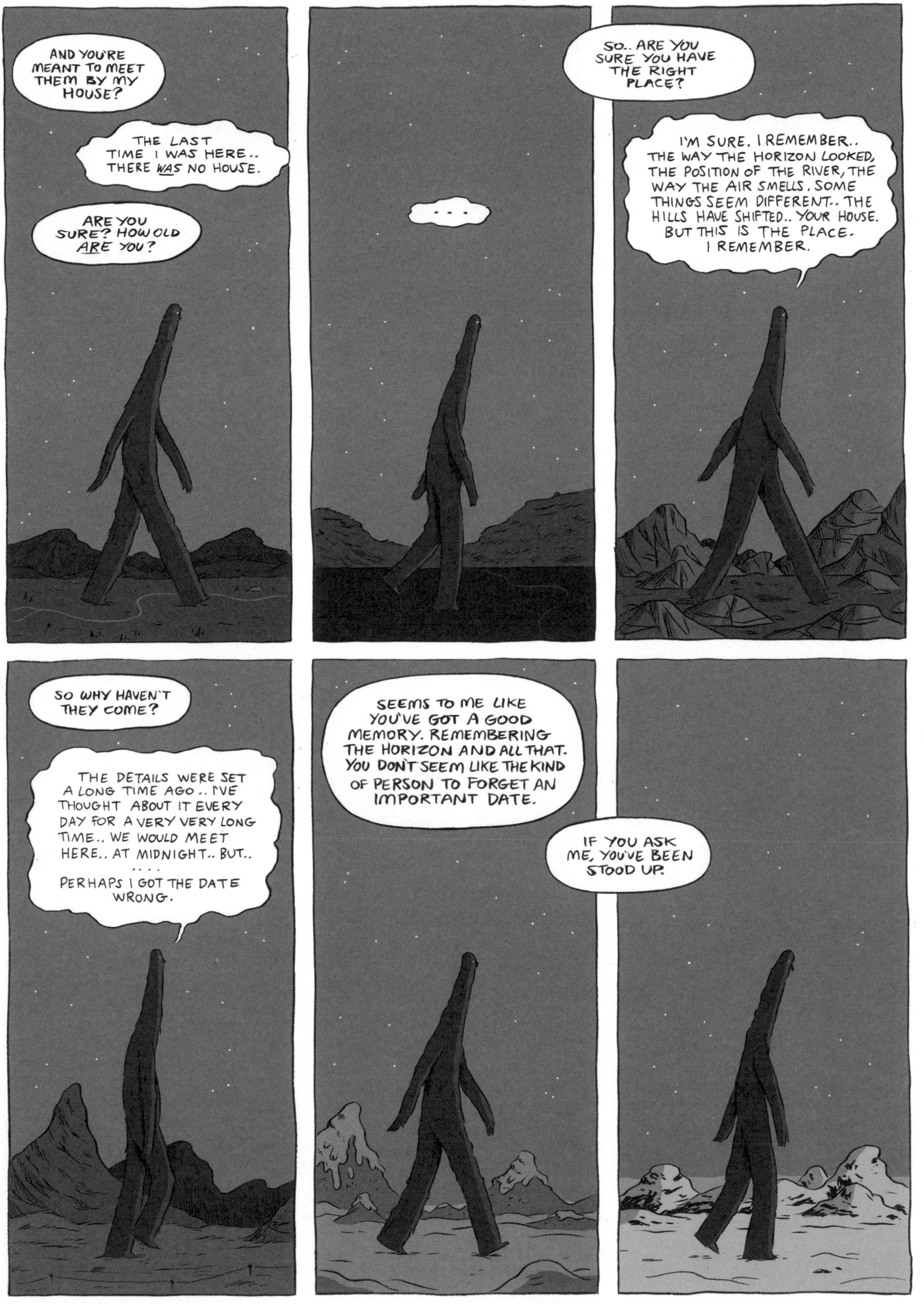
AND YOU'RE MEANT TO MEET THEM BY MY HOUSE?
THE LAST TIME I WAS HERE.. THERE WAS NO HOUSE.
ARE YOU SURE? HOW OLD ARE YOU?
. . .
SO.. ARE YOU SURE YOU HAVE THE RIGHT PLACE?
I'M SURE. I REMEMBER.. THE WAY THE HORIZON LOOKED, THE POSITION OF THE RIVER, THE WAY THE AIR SMELLS. SOME THINGS SEEM DIFFERENT.. THE HILLS HAVE SHIFTED.. YOUR HOUSE. BUT THIS IS THE PLACE. I REMEMBER.
SO WHY HAVEN'T THEY COME?
THE DETAILS WERE SET A LONG TIME AGO.. I'VE THOUGHT ABOUT IT EVERY DAY FOR A VERY VERY LONG TIME.. WE WOULD MEET HERE.. AT MIDNIGHT.. BUT.. . . . . PERHAPS I GOT THE DATE WRONG.
SEEMS TO ME LIKE YOU'VE GOT A GOOD MEMORY. REMEMBERING THE HORIZON AND ALL THAT. YOU DON'T SEEM LIKE THE KIND OF PERSON TO FORGET AN IMPORTANT DATE.
IF YOU ASK ME, YOU'VE BEEN STOOD UP.

I DON'T SEE THE SENSE IN COMING BACK HERE NIGHT AFTER NIGHT. YOU'VE GIVEN THEM ENOUGH TIME.

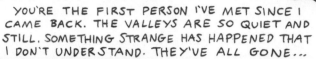

YOU'RE THE FIRST PERSON I'VE MET SINCE I CAME BACK. THE VALLEYS ARE SO QUIET AND STILL. SOMETHING STRANGE HAS HAPPENED THAT I DON'T UNDERSTAND. THEY'VE ALL GONE...

PERHAPS YOU'RE RIGHT.

PERHAPS SHE HAS TOO.

SHE?

IT WAS NICE TO FINALLY MEET YOU PROPERLY. AND THANKS FOR THE WALK.

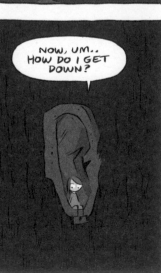
NOW, UM... HOW DO I GET DOWN?

CLIMB ONTO MY HAND.

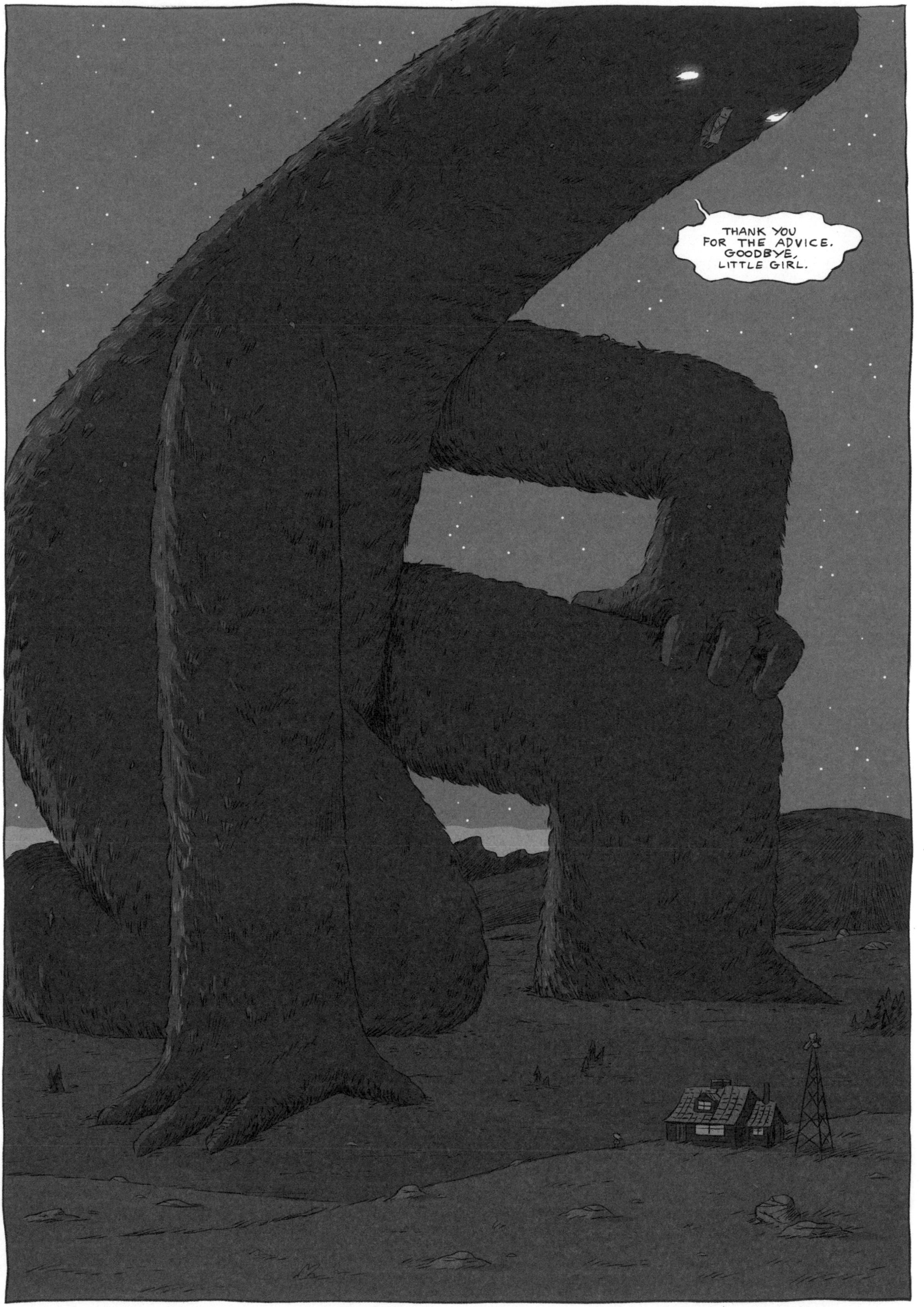
THANK YOU FOR THE ADVICE. GOODBYE, LITTLE GIRL.

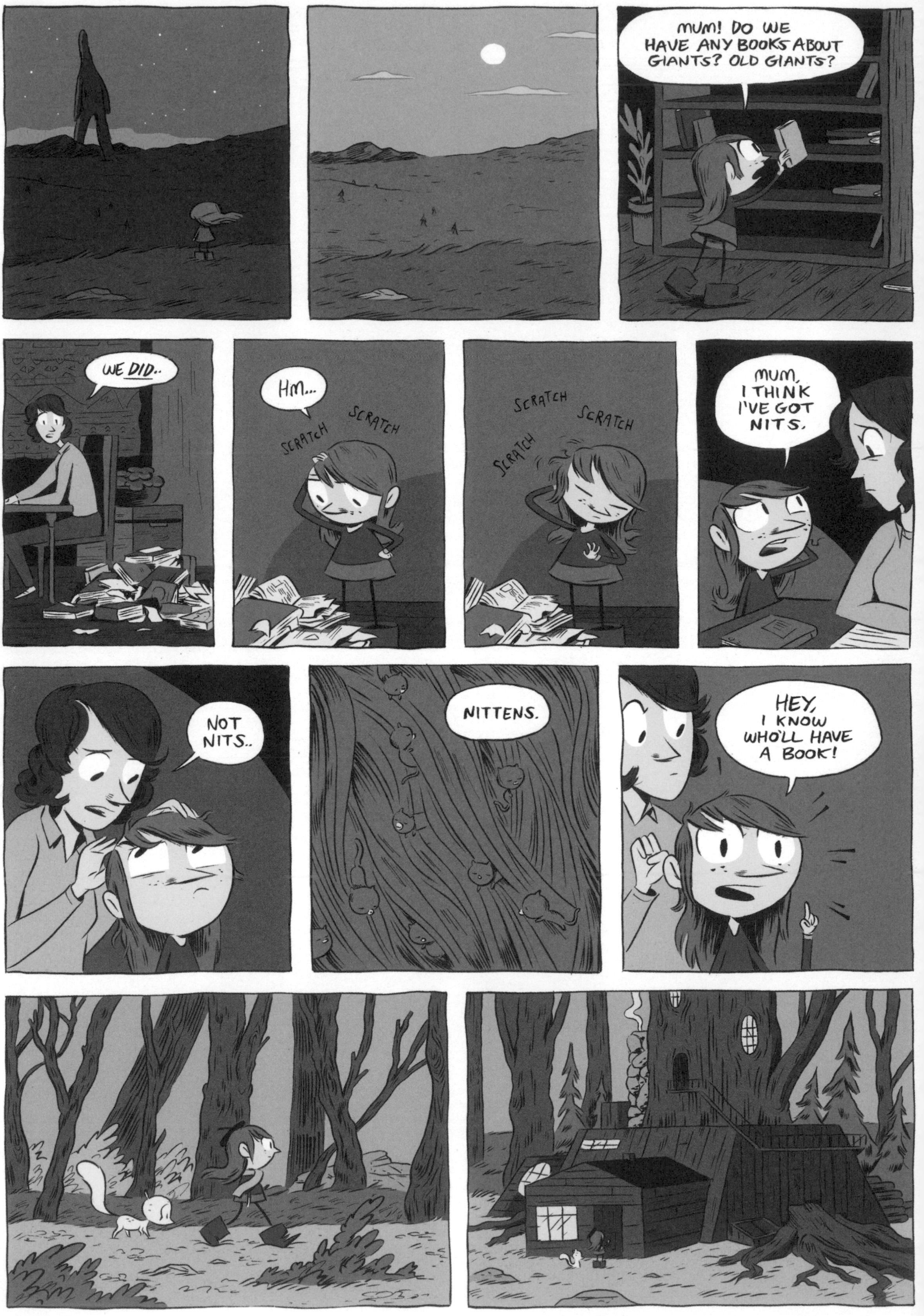
MUM! DO WE HAVE ANY BOOKS ABOUT GIANTS? OLD GIANTS?
WE DID..
HM...
SCRATCH
SCRATCH
SCRATCH
SCRATCH
SCRATCH
MUM, I THINK I'VE GOT NITS.
NOT NITS..
NITTENS.
HEY, I KNOW WHO'LL HAVE A BOOK!

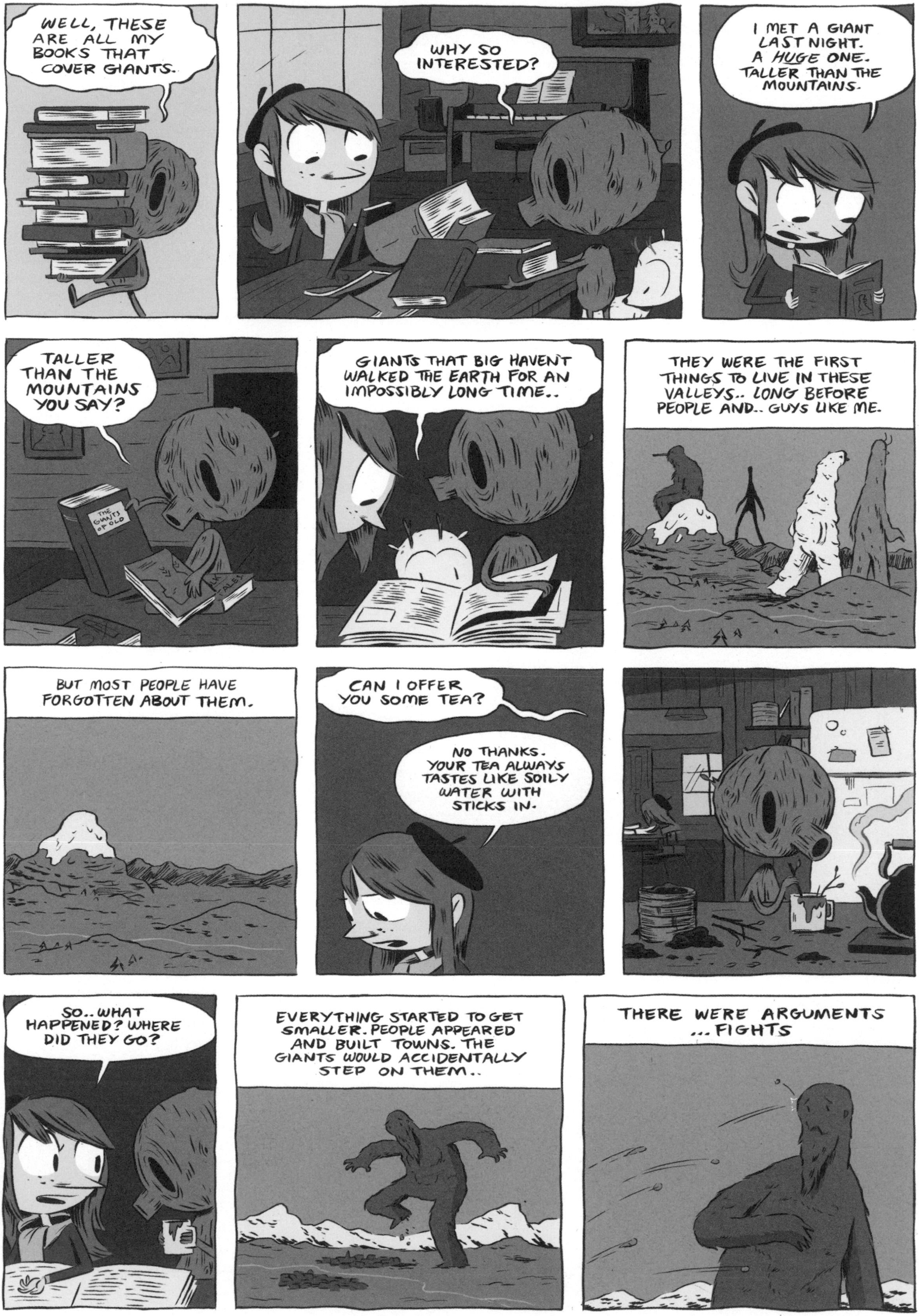
WELL, THESE ARE ALL MY BOOKS THAT COVER GIANTS.
WHY SO INTERESTED?
I MET A GIANT LAST NIGHT. A HUGE ONE. TALLER THAN THE MOUNTAINS.
TALLER THAN THE MOUNTAINS YOU SAY?
THE GIANTS OF OLD
GIANTS THAT BIG HAVEN'T WALKED THE EARTH FOR AN IMPOSSIBLY LONG TIME..
THEY WERE THE FIRST THINGS TO LIVE IN THESE VALLEYS.. LONG BEFORE PEOPLE AND.. GUYS LIKE ME.
BUT MOST PEOPLE HAVE FORGOTTEN ABOUT THEM.
CAN I OFFER YOU SOME TEA?
NO THANKS. YOUR TEA ALWAYS TASTES LIKE SOILY WATER WITH STICKS IN.
SO.. WHAT HAPPENED? WHERE DID THEY GO?
EVERYTHING STARTED TO GET SMALLER. PEOPLE APPEARED AND BUILT TOWNS. THE GIANTS WOULD ACCIDENTALLY STEP ON THEM..
THERE WERE ARGUMENTS ...FIGHTS

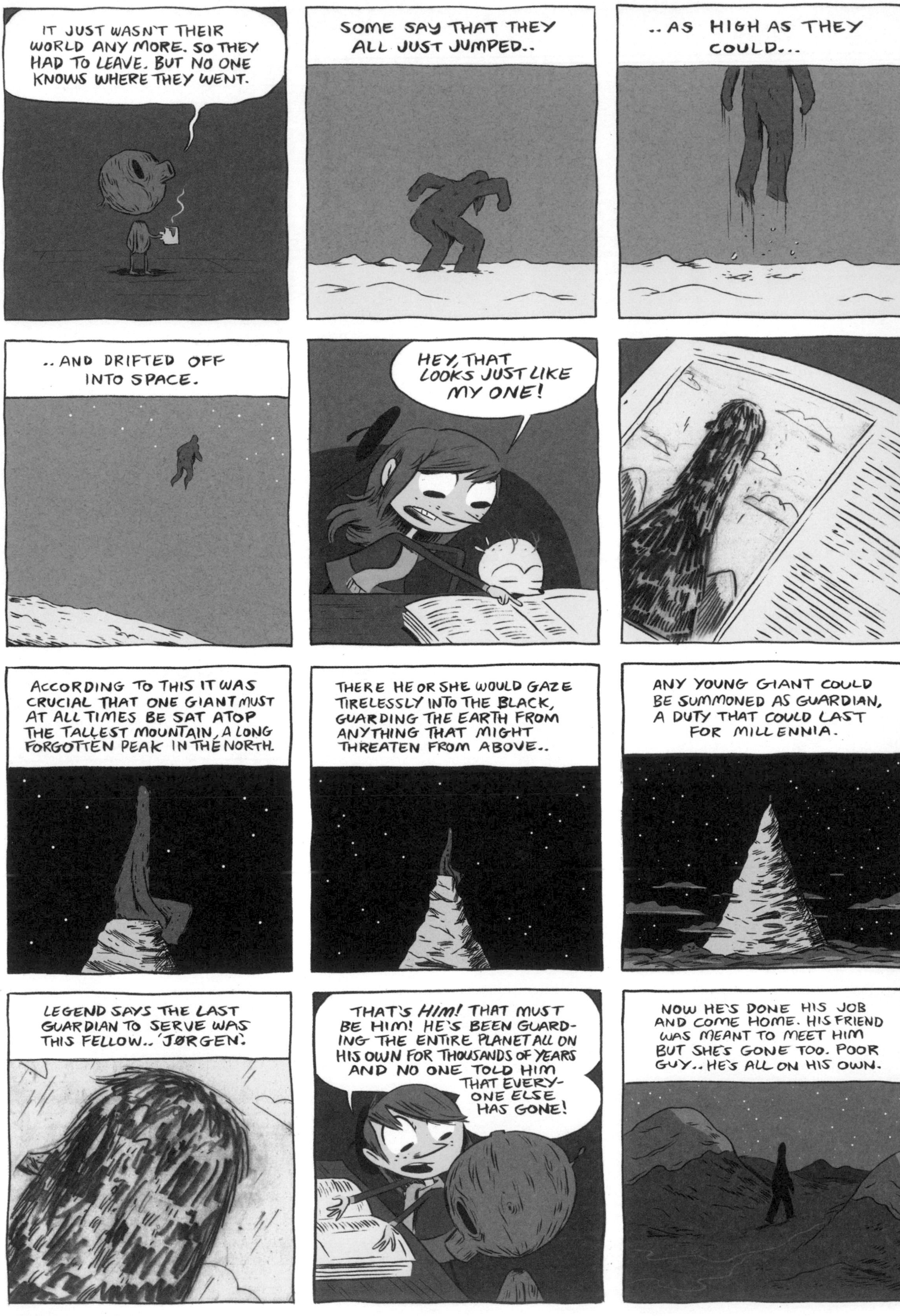
IT JUST WASN'T THEIR WORLD ANY MORE. SO THEY HAD TO LEAVE. BUT NO ONE KNOWS WHERE THEY WENT.
SOME SAY THAT THEY ALL JUST JUMPED..
..AS HIGH AS THEY COULD...
..AND DRIFTED OFF INTO SPACE.
HEY, THAT LOOKS JUST LIKE MY ONE!
ACCORDING TO THIS IT WAS CRUCIAL THAT ONE GIANT MUST AT ALL TIMES BE SAT ATOP THE TALLEST MOUNTAIN, A LONG FORGOTTEN PEAK IN THE NORTH.
THERE HE OR SHE WOULD GAZE TIRELESSLY INTO THE BLACK, GUARDING THE EARTH FROM ANYTHING THAT MIGHT THREATEN FROM ABOVE..
ANY YOUNG GIANT COULD BE SUMMONED AS GUARDIAN, A DUTY THAT COULD LAST FOR MILLENNIA.
LEGEND SAYS THE LAST GUARDIAN TO SERVE WAS THIS FELLOW.. 'JØRGEN'.
THAT'S HIM! THAT MUST BE HIM! HE'S BEEN GUARDING THE ENTIRE PLANET ALL ON HIS OWN FOR THOUSANDS OF YEARS AND NO ONE TOLD HIM THAT EVERYONE ELSE HAS GONE!
NOW HE'S DONE HIS JOB AND COME HOME. HIS FRIEND WAS MEANT TO MEET HIM BUT SHE'S GONE TOO. POOR GUY.. HE'S ALL ON HIS OWN.

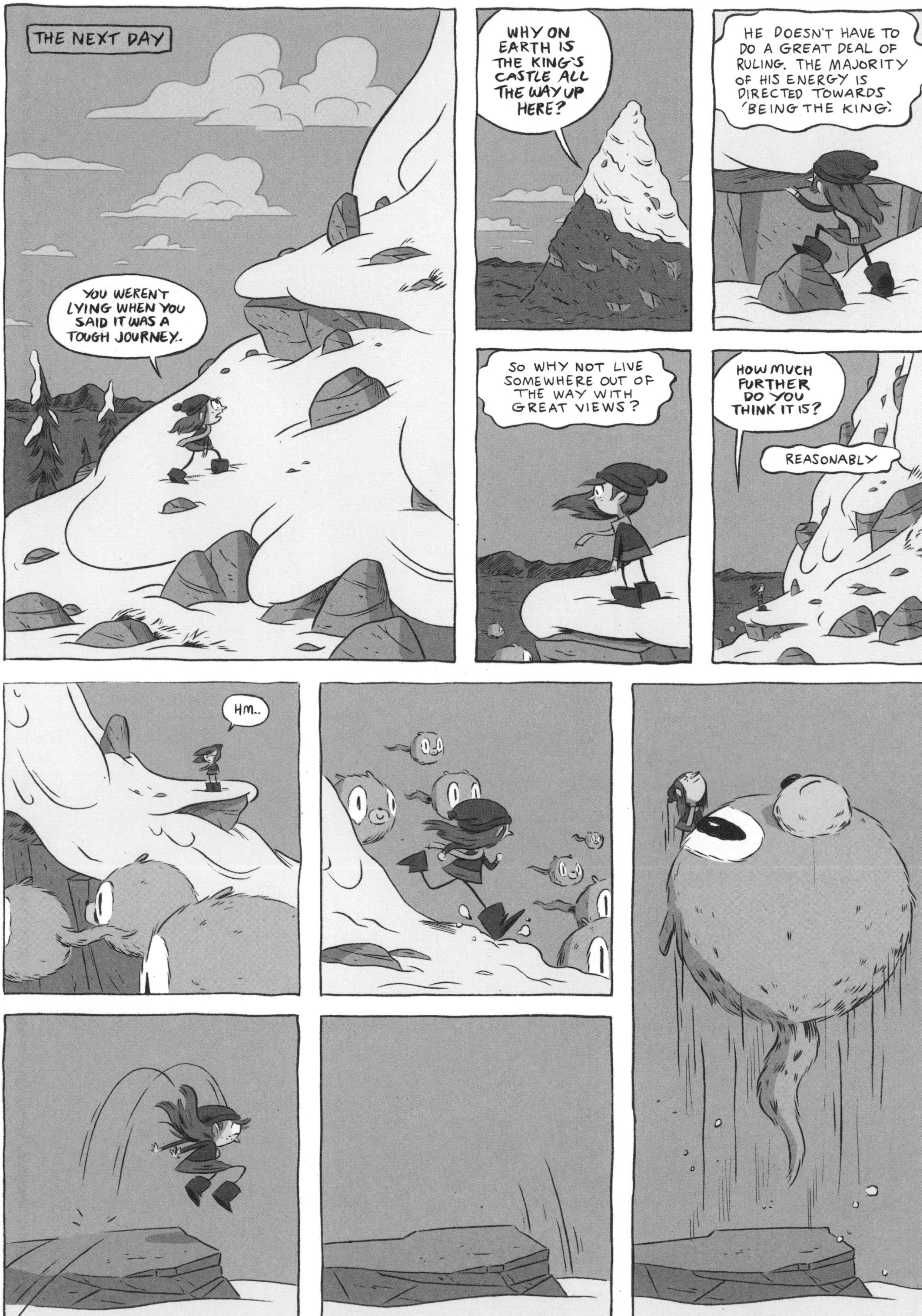
THE NEXT DAY
YOU WEREN'T LYING WHEN YOU SAID IT WAS A TOUGH JOURNEY..
WHY ON EARTH IS THE KING'S CASTLE ALL THE WAY UP HERE?
HE DOESN'T HAVE TO DO A GREAT DEAL OF RULING. THE MAJORITY OF HIS ENERGY IS DIRECTED TOWARDS 'BEING THE KING'.
SO WHY NOT LIVE SOMEWHERE OUT OF THE WAY WITH GREAT VIEWS?
HOW MUCH FURTHER DO YOU THINK IT IS?
REASONABLY
HM..

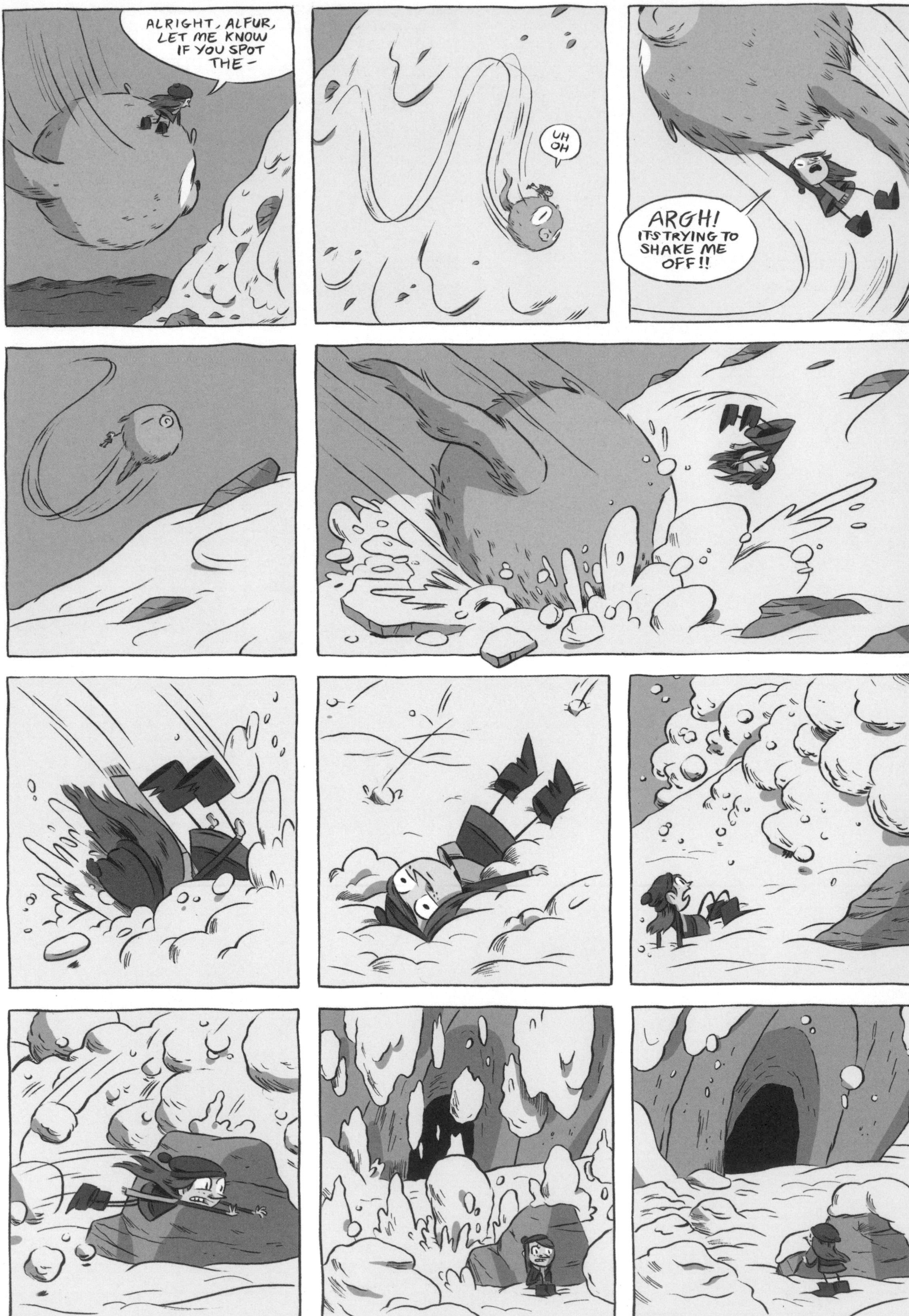
ALRIGHT, ALFUR, LET ME KNOW IF YOU SPOT THE-
UH OH
ARGH! ITS TRYING TO SHAKE ME OFF!!

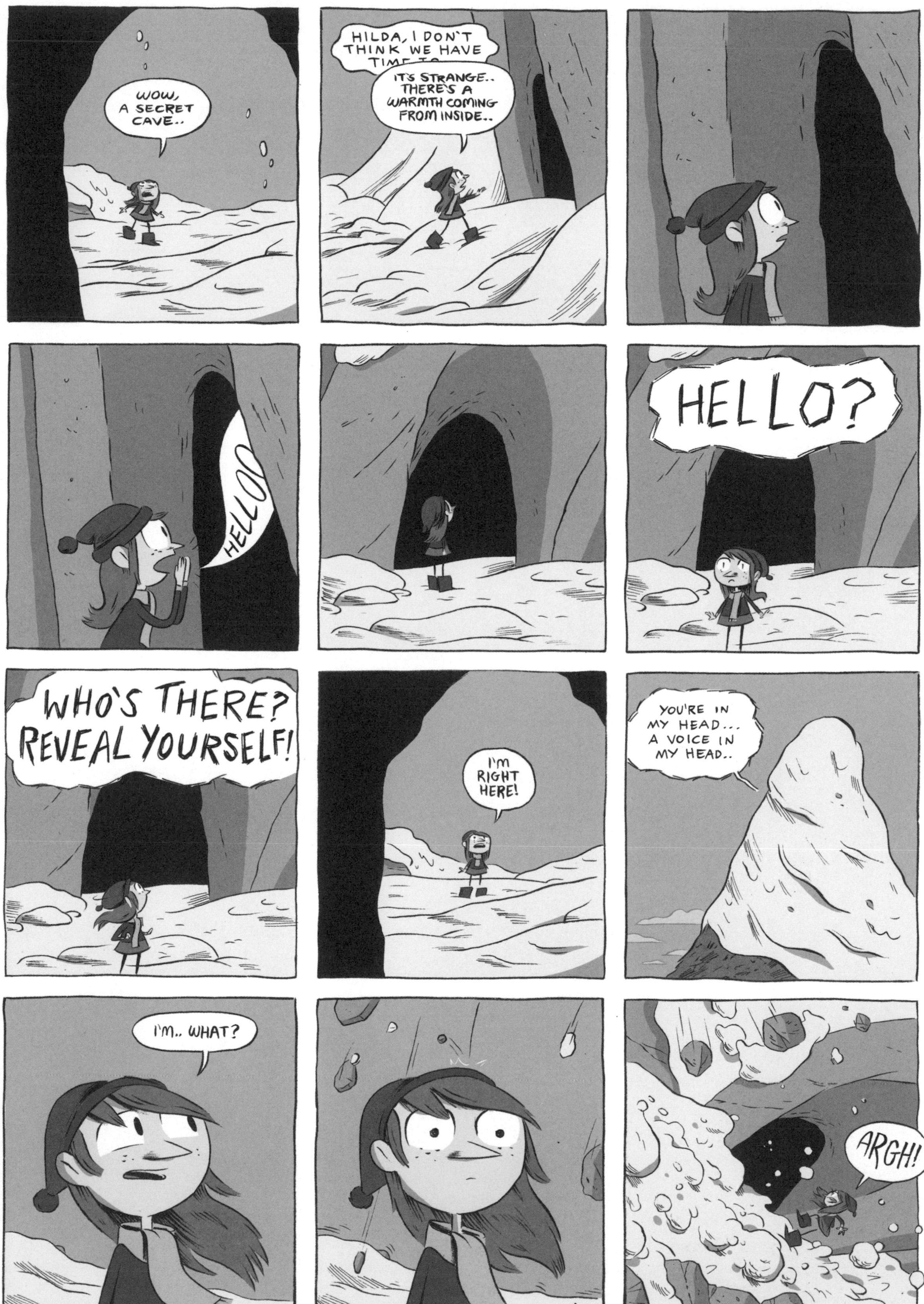
WOW, A SECRET CAVE..
HILDA, I DON'T THINK WE HAVE
IT'S STRANGE.. THERE'S A WARMTH COMING FROM INSIDE..
HELLOO
HELLO?
WHO'S THERE? REVEAL YOURSELF!
I'M RIGHT HERE!
YOU'RE IN MY HEAD... A VOICE IN MY HEAD..
I'M.. WHAT?
ARGH!

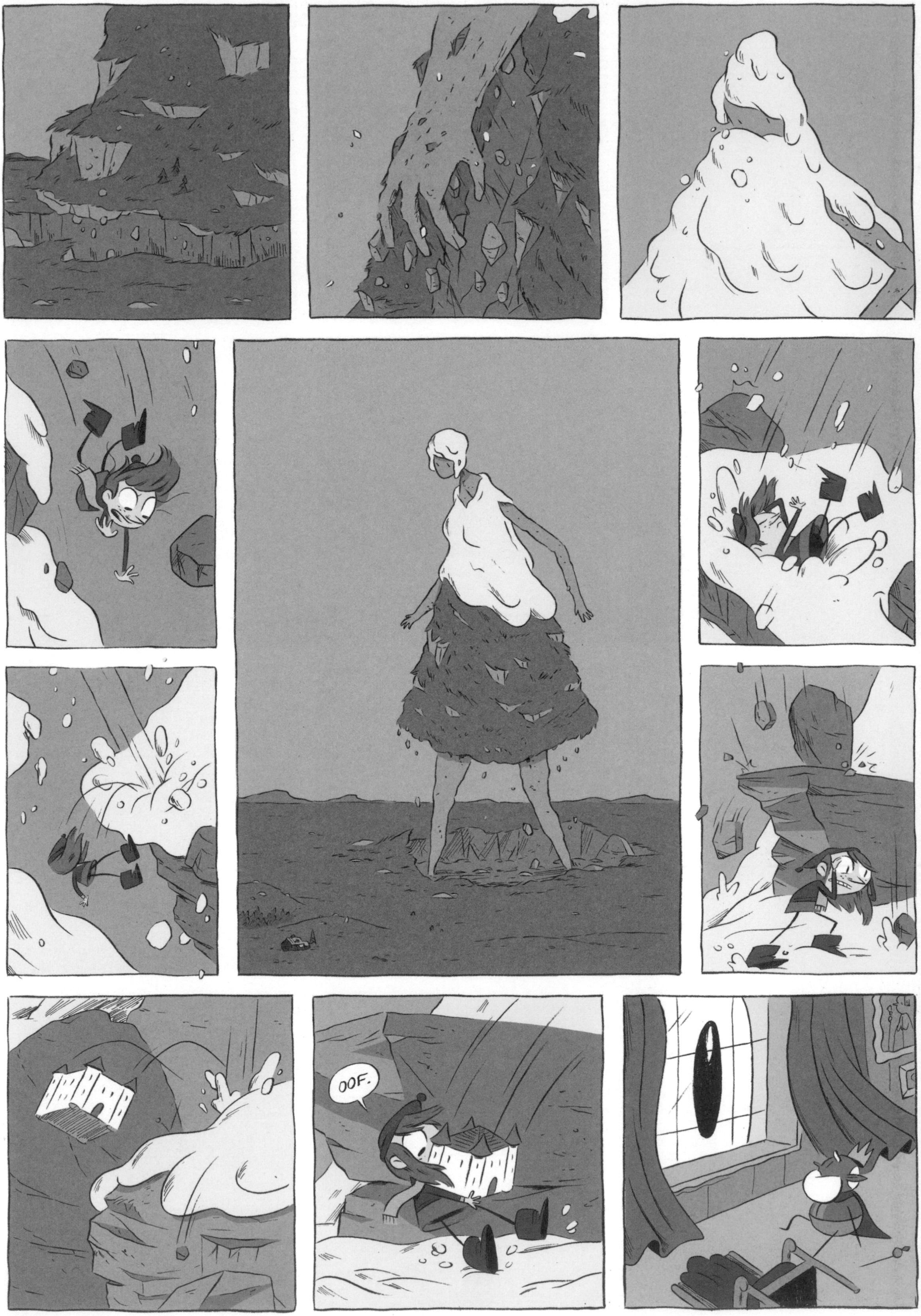
OOF.

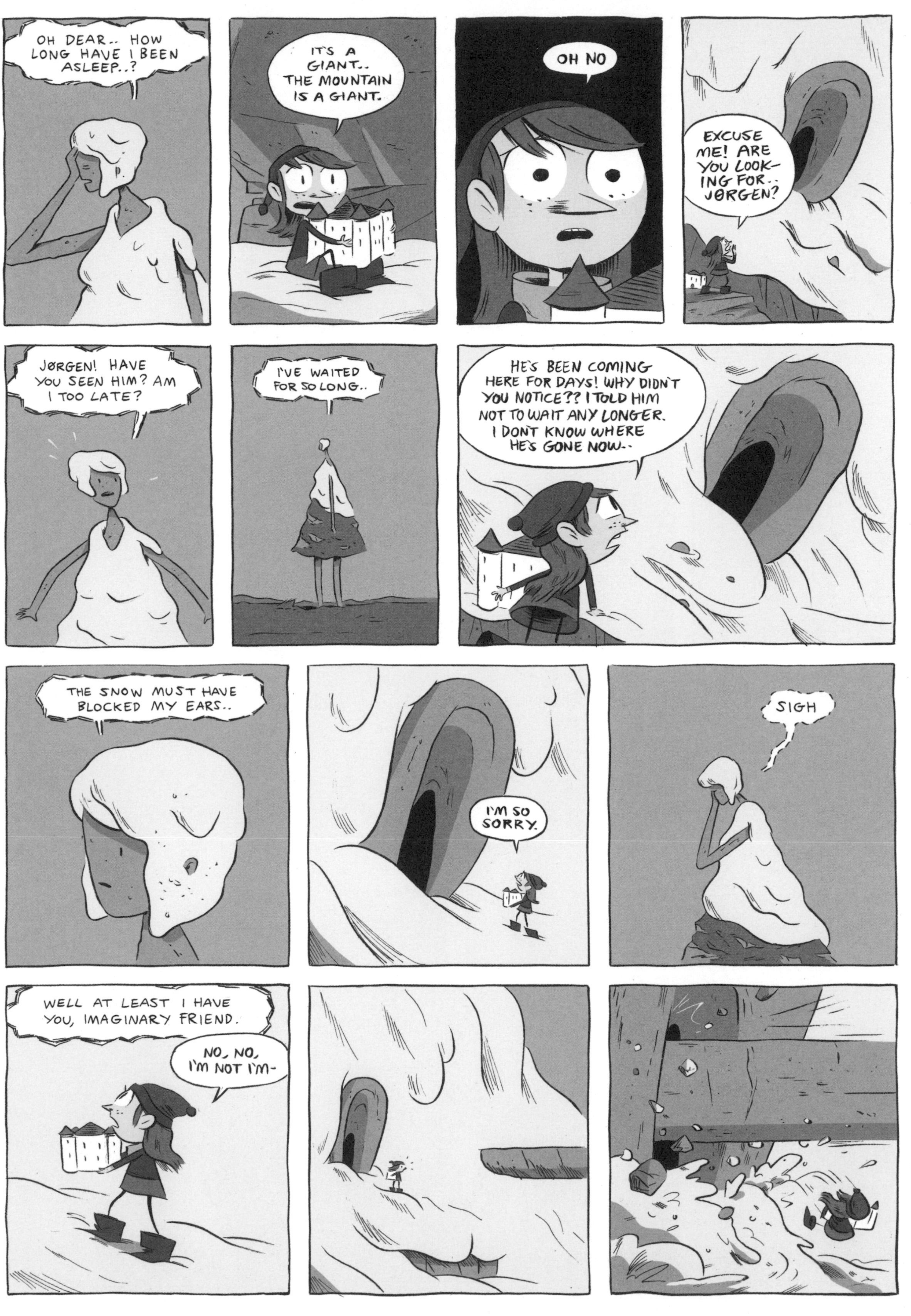

OH DEAR.. HOW LONG HAVE I BEEN ASLEEP..?
IT'S A GIANT.. THE MOUNTAIN IS A GIANT.
OH NO
EXCUSE ME! ARE YOU LOOKING FOR.. JØRGEN?
JØRGEN! HAVE YOU SEEN HIM? AM I TOO LATE?
I'VE WAITED FOR SO LONG..
HE'S BEEN COMING HERE FOR DAYS! WHY DIDN'T YOU NOTICE?? I TOLD HIM NOT TO WAIT ANY LONGER. I DON'T KNOW WHERE HE'S GONE NOW..
THE SNOW MUST HAVE BLOCKED MY EARS..
I'M SO SORRY.
SIGH
WELL AT LEAST I HAVE YOU, IMAGINARY FRIEND.
NO, NO, I'M NOT I'M-

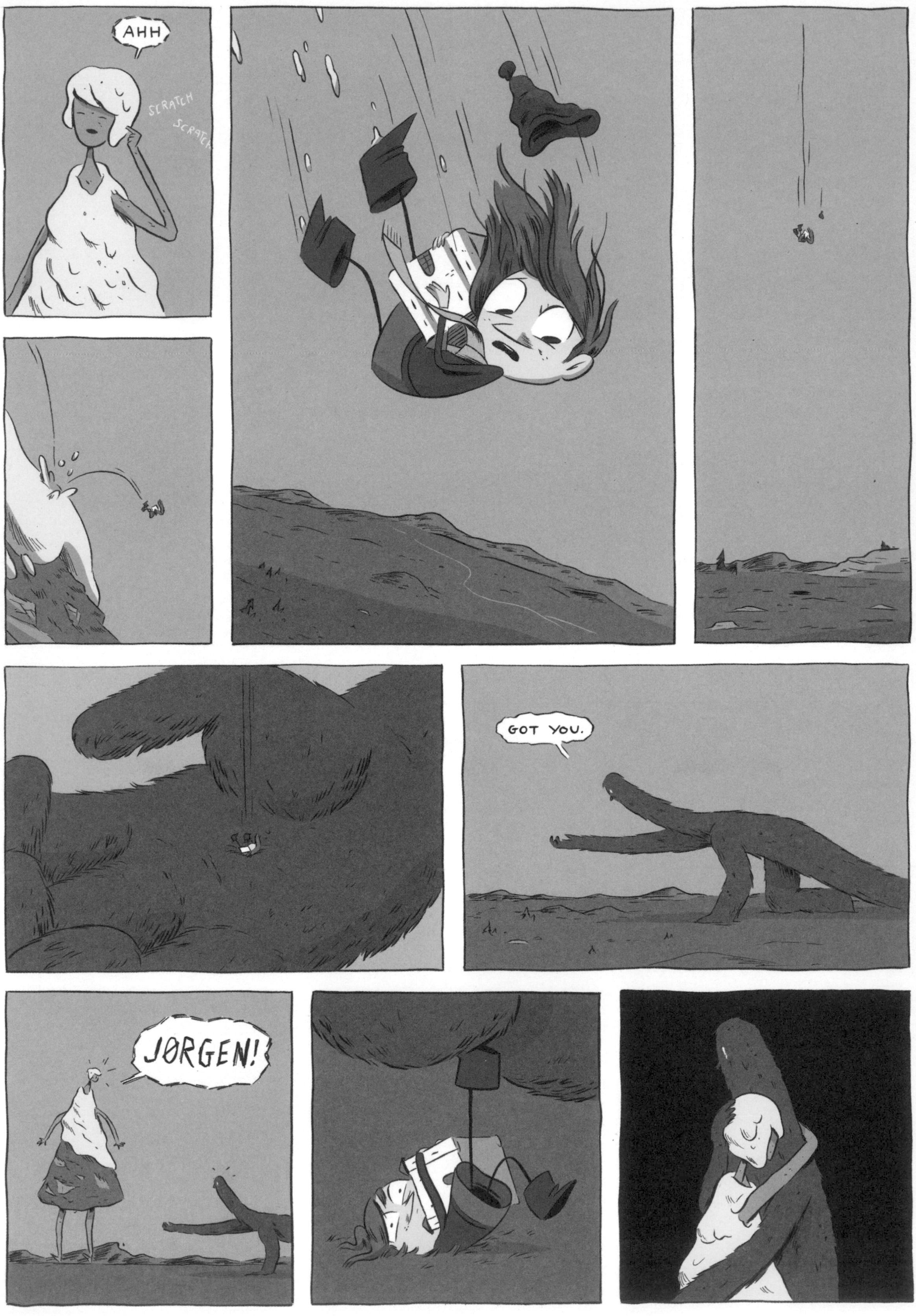
AHH
SCRATCH
SCRATCH
GOT YOU.
JØRGEN!

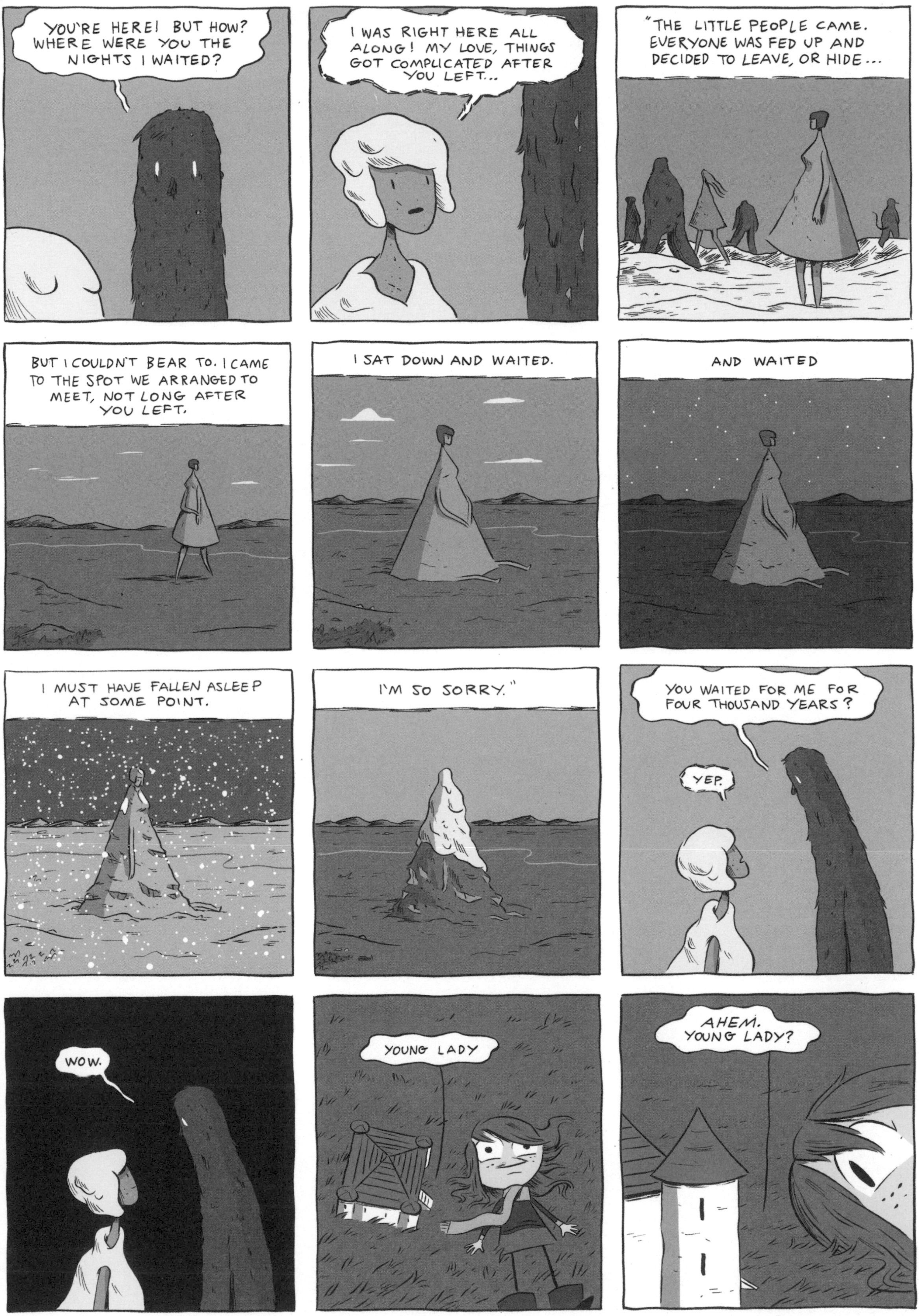

YOU'RE HERE! BUT HOW? WHERE WERE YOU THE NIGHTS I WAITED?
I WAS RIGHT HERE ALL ALONG! MY LOVE, THINGS GOT COMPLICATED AFTER YOU LEFT...
"THE LITTLE PEOPLE CAME. EVERYONE WAS FED UP AND DECIDED TO LEAVE, OR HIDE...
BUT I COULDN'T BEAR TO. I CAME TO THE SPOT WE ARRANGED TO MEET, NOT LONG AFTER YOU LEFT.
I SAT DOWN AND WAITED.
AND WAITED
I MUST HAVE FALLEN ASLEEP AT SOME POINT.
I'M SO SORRY."
YOU WAITED FOR ME FOR FOUR THOUSAND YEARS?
YEP.
WOW.
YOUNG LADY
AHEM. YOUNG LADY?

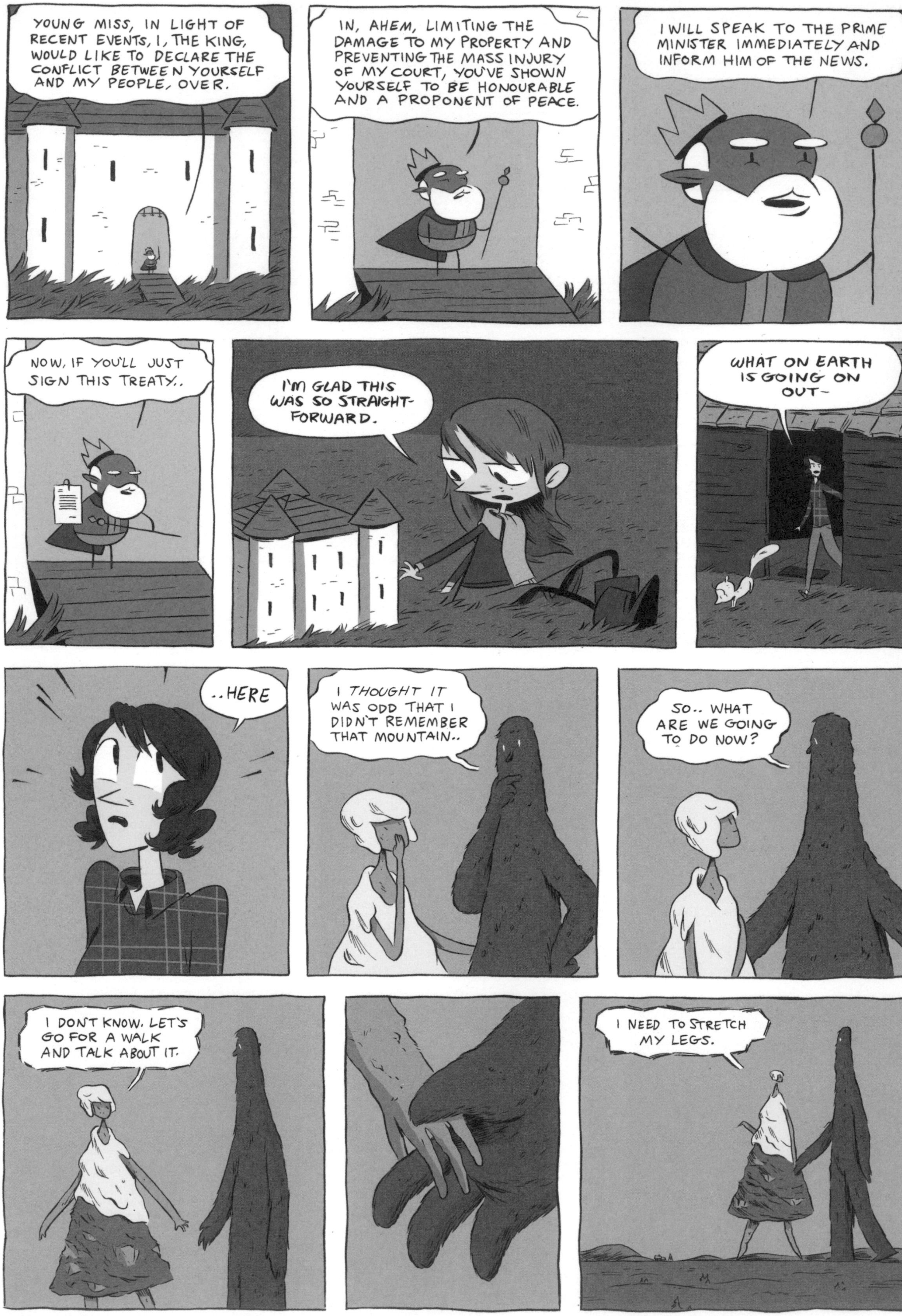
YOUNG MISS, IN LIGHT OF RECENT EVENTS, I, THE KING, WOULD LIKE TO DECLARE THE CONFLICT BETWEEN YOURSELF AND MY PEOPLE, OVER.
IN, AHEM, LIMITING THE DAMAGE TO MY PROPERTY AND PREVENTING THE MASS INJURY OF MY COURT, YOU'VE SHOWN YOURSELF TO BE HONOURABLE AND A PROPONENT OF PEACE.
I WILL SPEAK TO THE PRIME MINISTER IMMEDIATELY AND INFORM HIM OF THE NEWS.
NOW, IF YOU'LL JUST SIGN THIS TREATY..
I'M GLAD THIS WAS SO STRAIGHT-FORWARD.
WHAT ON EARTH IS GOING ON OUT-
..HERE
I THOUGHT IT WAS ODD THAT I DIDN'T REMEMBER THAT MOUNTAIN..
SO.. WHAT ARE WE GOING TO DO NOW?
I DON'T KNOW. LET'S GO FOR A WALK AND TALK ABOUT IT.
I NEED TO STRETCH MY LEGS.

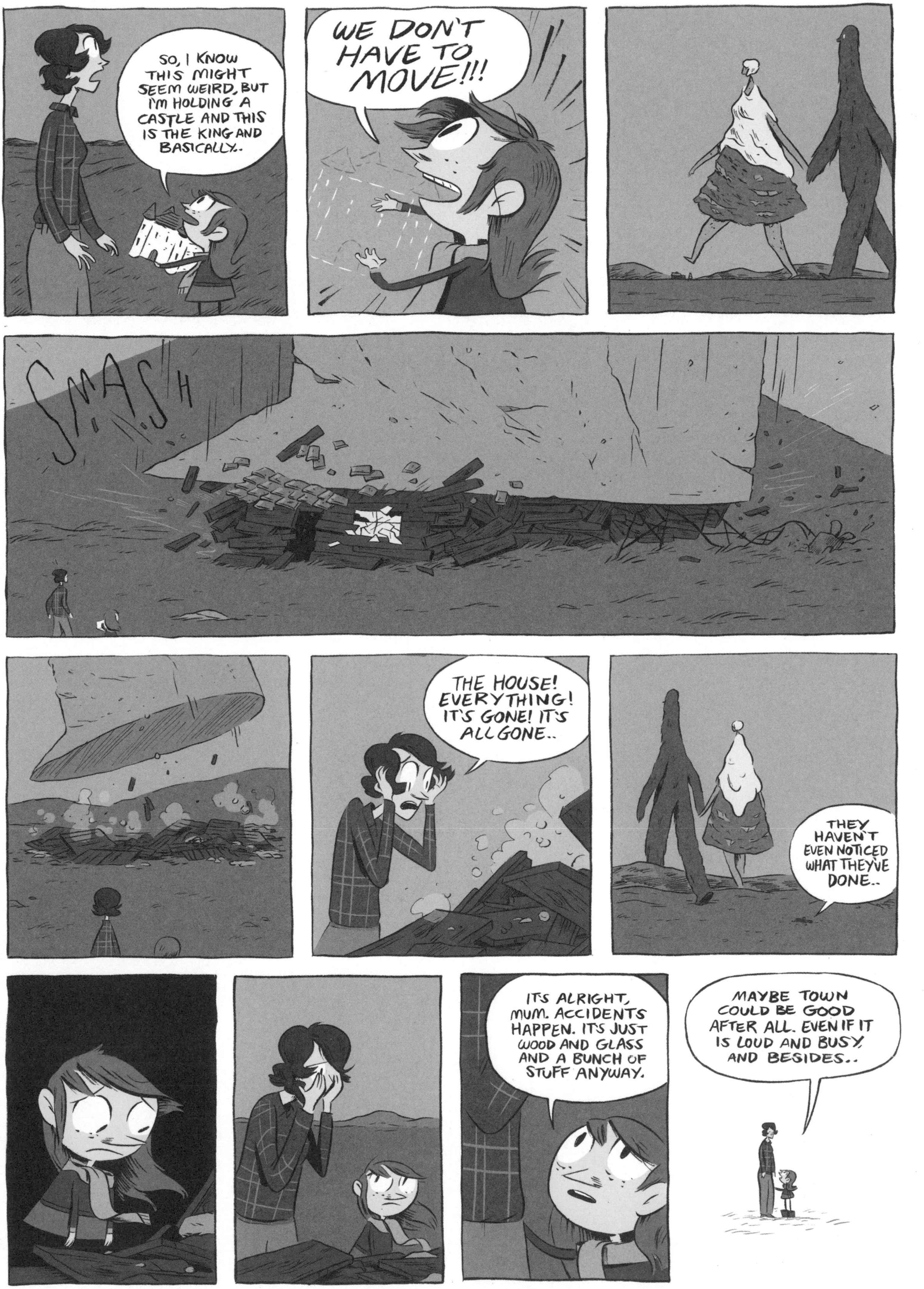
SO, I KNOW THIS MIGHT SEEM WEIRD, BUT I'M HOLDING A CASTLE AND THIS IS THE KING AND BASICALLY..
WE DON'T HAVE TO MOVE!!!
SMASH
THE HOUSE! EVERYTHING! IT'S GONE! IT'S ALL GONE..
THEY HAVEN'T EVEN NOTICED WHAT THEY'VE DONE..
IT'S ALRIGHT, MUM. ACCIDENTS HAPPEN. IT'S JUST WOOD AND GLASS AND A BUNCH OF STUFF ANYWAY.
MAYBE TOWN COULD BE GOOD AFTER ALL. EVEN IF IT IS LOUD AND BUSY, AND BESIDES..

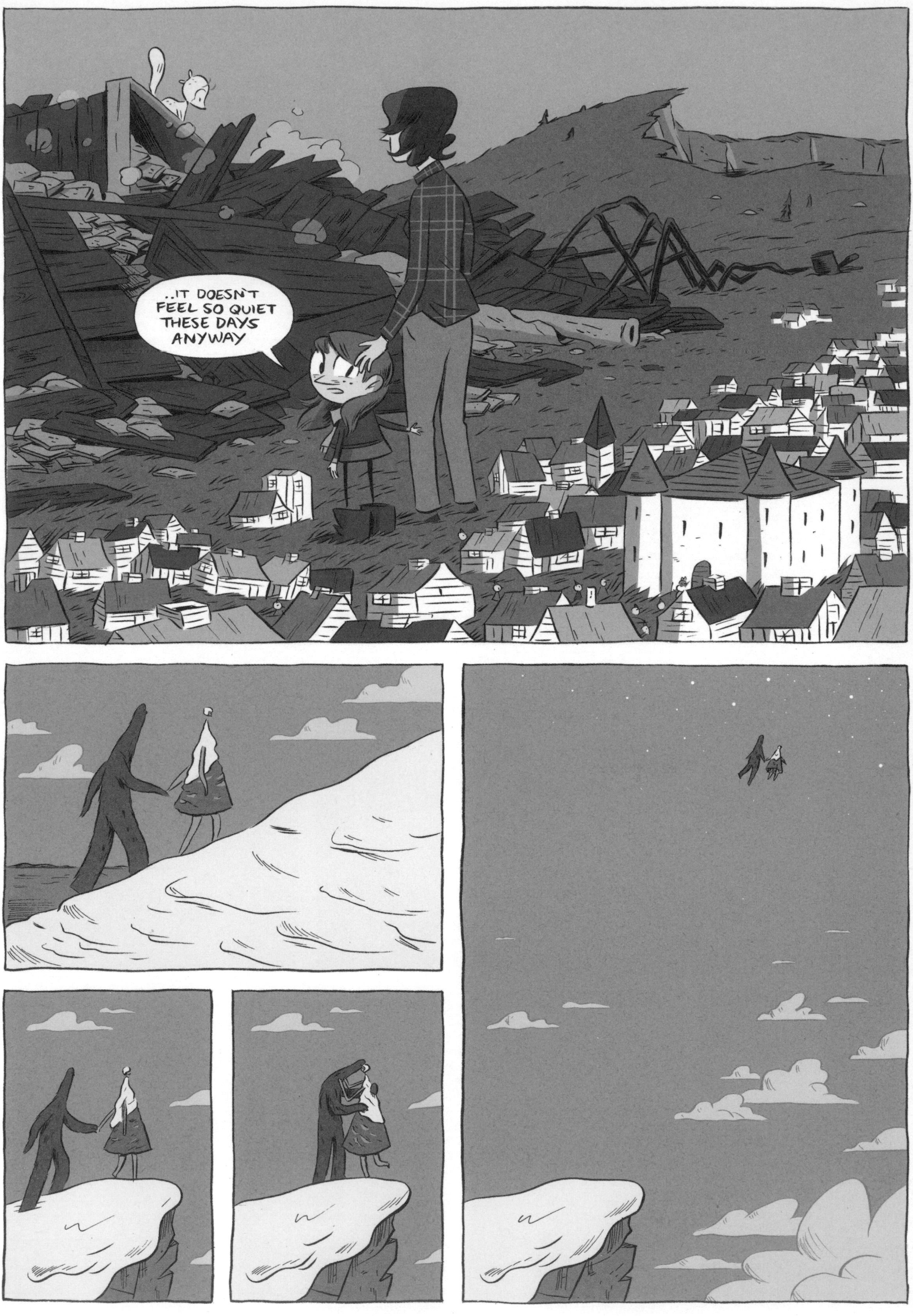
..IT DOESN'T FEEL SO QUIET THESE DAYS ANYWAY

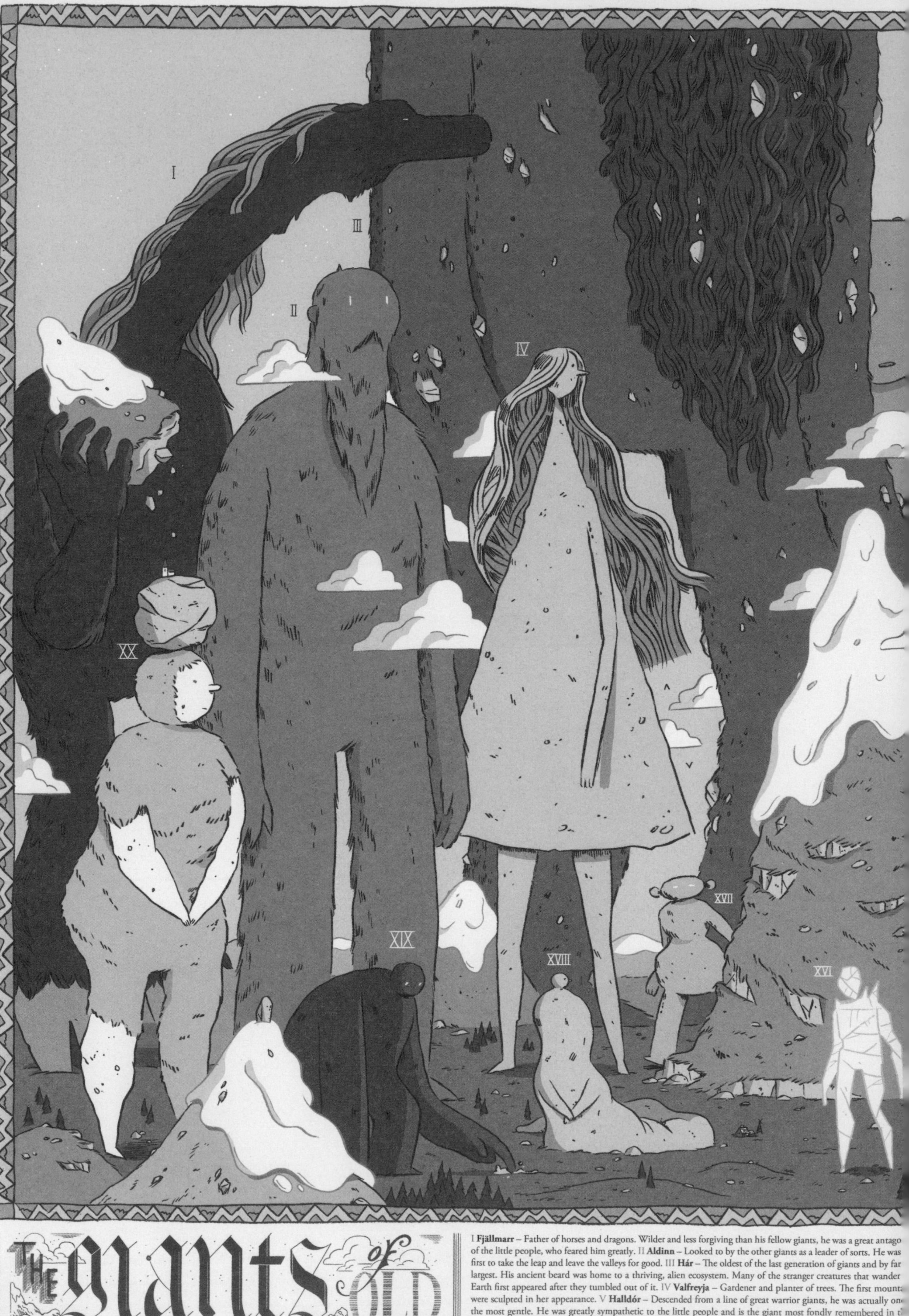

I
III
II
IV
V
XX
XVII
XIX
XVIII
XVI

The Giants of Old

I **Fjällmarr** – Father of horses and dragons. Wilder and less forgiving than his fellow giants, he was a great antago of the little people, who feared him greatly. II **Aldinn** – Looked to by the other giants as a leader of sorts. He was first to take the leap and leave the valleys for good. III **Hár** – The oldest of the last generation of giants and by far largest. His ancient beard was home to a thriving, alien ecosystem. Many of the stranger creatures that wander Earth first appeared after they tumbled out of it. IV **Valfreyja** – Gardener and planter of trees. The first mount were sculpted in her appearance. V **Halldór** – Descended from a line of great warrior giants, he was actually on the most gentle. He was greatly sympathetic to the little people and is the giant most fondly remembered in t tales. He did not leave with the others and it is unclear what became of him. VI **Jørgen** - The last guard

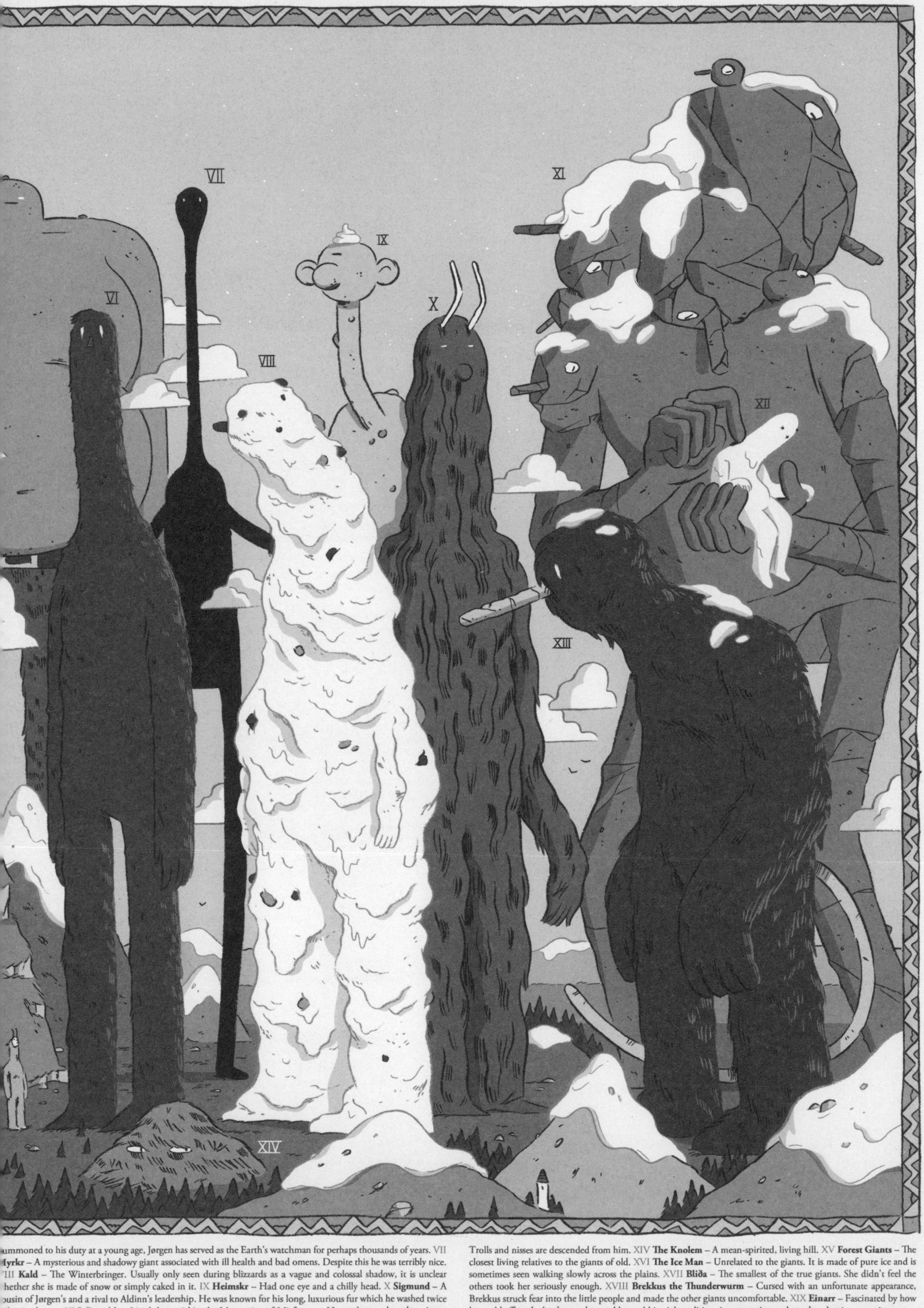

VII
XI
IX
VI
X
VIII
XII
XIII
XIV

ummoned to his duty at a young age, Jørgen has served as the Earth's watchman for perhaps thousands of years. VII **lyrkr** – A mysterious and shadowy giant associated with ill health and bad omens. Despite this he was terribly nice. III **Kald** – The Winterbringer. Usually only seen during blizzards as a vague and colossal shadow, it is unclear hether she is made of snow or simply caked in it. IX **Heimskr** – Had one eye and a chilly head. X **Sigmund** – A ousin of Jørgen's and a rival to Aldinn's leadership. He was known for his long, luxurious fur which he washed twice day in the sea. XI **Jaðarrokk** – Lived deep within the Mountains of Misfortune. He rarely saw the other giants, referring the company of his six extra heads. XII **Drib** – Kald's older (yet smaller) brother. XIII **Björg** – The outcast f the group. He was fearful of the other giants and not well liked. When the others left he went into hiding. Trolls and nisses are descended from him. XIV **The Knolem** – A mean-spirited, living hill. XV **Forest Giants** – The closest living relatives to the giants of old. XVI **The Ice Man** – Unrelated to the giants. It is made of pure ice and is sometimes seen walking slowly across the plains. XVII **Blíða** – The smallest of the true giants. She didn't feel the others took her seriously enough. XVIII **Brekkus the Thunderwurm** – Cursed with an unfortunate appearance, Brekkus struck fear into the little people and made the other giants uncomfortable. XIX **Einarr** – Fascinated by how he could affect the landscape, he would spend his nights editing rivers, moving rocks and replanting trees, just to see how the people would react in the morning. XX **Gertl** – The smartest giant and the most fun to be around. She once decided to see how long she could balance an enormous boulder on her head. The legends say that it never fell off.

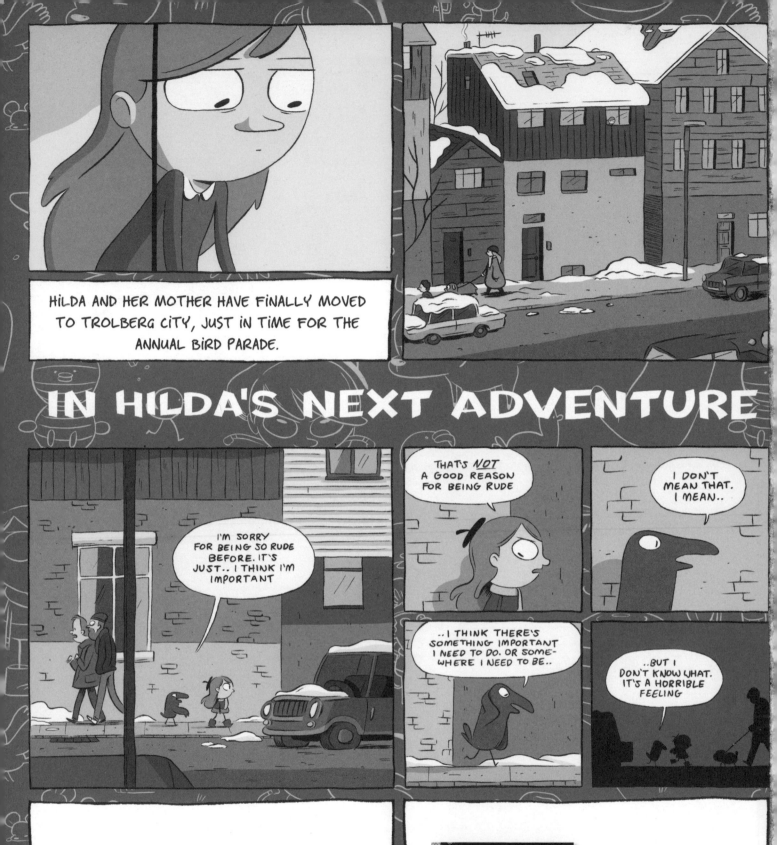

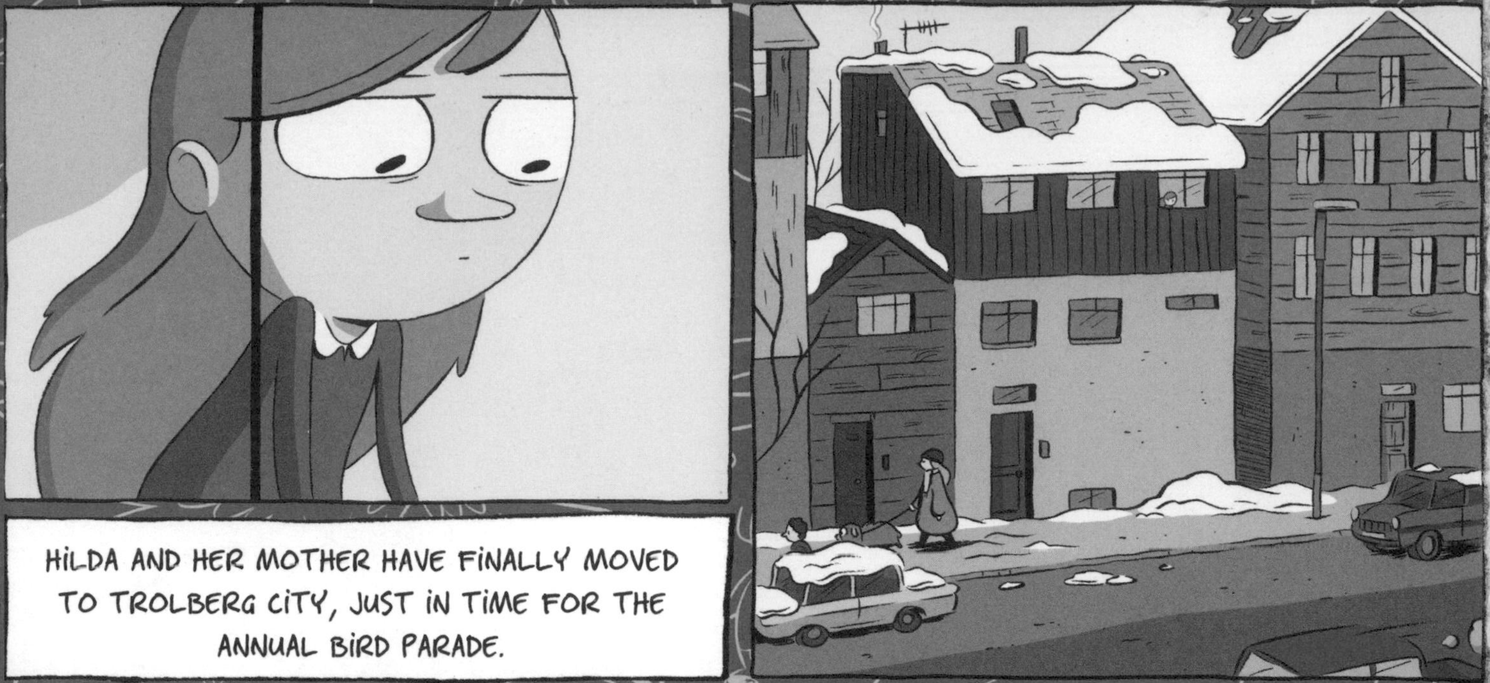
HILDA AND HER MOTHER HAVE FINALLY MOVED TO TROLBERG CITY, JUST IN TIME FOR THE ANNUAL BIRD PARADE.

IN HILDA'S NEXT ADVENTURE

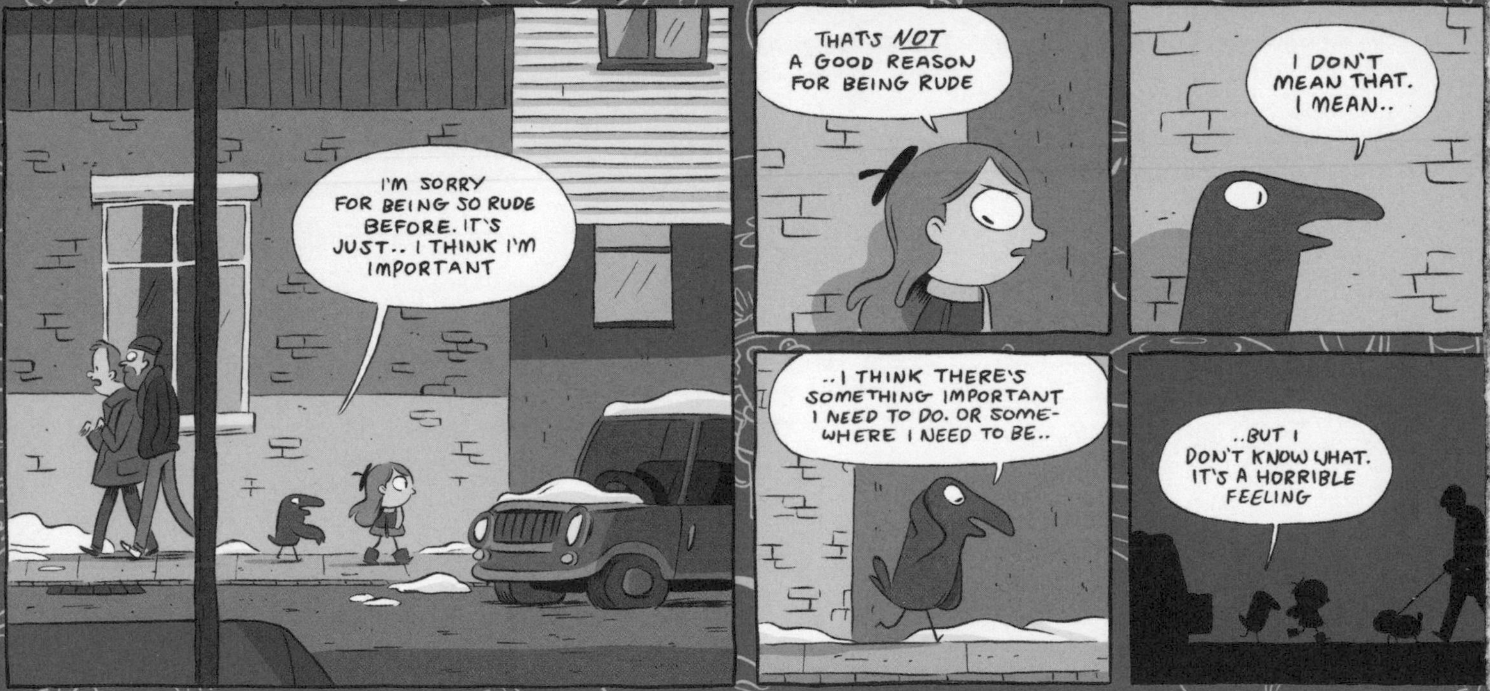
I'M SORRY FOR BEING SO RUDE BEFORE. IT'S JUST.. I THINK I'M IMPORTANT
THAT'S NOT A GOOD REASON FOR BEING RUDE
I DON'T MEAN THAT. I MEAN..
..I THINK THERE'S SOMETHING IMPORTANT I NEED TO DO. OR SOMEWHERE I NEED TO BE..
..BUT I DON'T KNOW WHAT. IT'S A HORRIBLE FEELING

WHEN HILDA RESCUES AN INJURED RAVEN, SHE REALISES HER NEW WARD IS NO ORDINARY BIRD... IT HAS THE ABILITY TO SHIFT FORM.

WHAT'S THE MEANING OF IT ALL? WILL THE SECRET BE REVEALED AT THE BIRD PARADE?

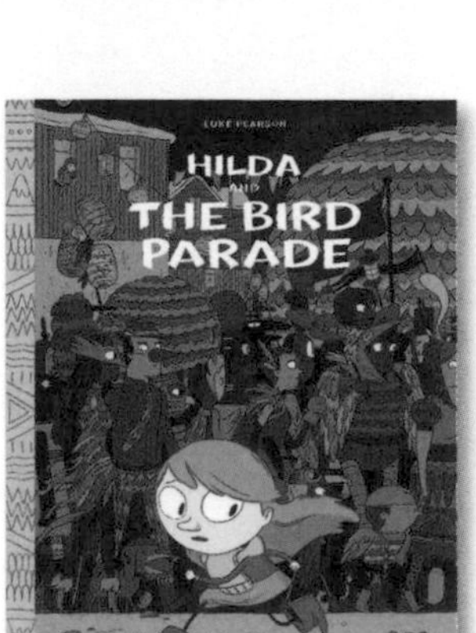
LUKE PEARSON
HILDA AND THE BIRD PARADE
FLYING EYE BOOKS

ISBN 978-1-909263-79-6

ORDER FROM WWW.FLYINGEYEBOOKS.COM OR ALL GOOD BOOKSHOPS